A Mountain to the North,
a Lake to the South,
Paths to the West,
a River to the Ea

LÁSZLÓ KRASZNAHORKAI

A Mountain to the North,
a Lake to the South,
Paths to the West,
a River to the East

translated from the Hungarian by Ottilie Mulzet

A NEW DIRECTIONS PAPERBOOK ORIGINAL

Originally published in Hungarian as *Északról hegy, Délről tó,*
Nyugatról utak, Keletről folyó, by Magvető Kiadó, Budapest.

The translator would like to thank the Hungarian Translators' House
in Balatonfüred, Hungary, for their kind support through their Home Office program.

The Publisher would like to thank David Trubatch for his assistance
with the mathematical section of this book.

Manufactured in the United States of America
First published as New Directions Paperbook 1547 in 2022
Design by Erik Rieselbach

Library of Congress Cataloging-in-Publication Data
Names: Krasznahorkai, László, author. | Mulzet, Ottilie, translator.
Title: A mountain to the North, a lake to the South,
paths to the West, a river to the East / by László Krasznahorkai ;
translated from the Hungarian by Ottilie Mulzet.
Description: First edition. | New York : New Directions Publishing, 2022.
Identifiers: LCCN 2022018692 | ISBN 9780811234474 (paperback) |
ISBN 9780811234481 (ebook)
Classification: LCC PH3281.K8866 M68 2022 | DDC 892.8—dc23/eng/20220418
LC record available at https://lccn.loc.gov/2022018692

2 4 6 8 10 9 7 5 3 1

New Directions Books are published for James Laughlin
by New Directions Publishing Corporation
80 Eighth Avenue, New York 10011

None saw it twice

A Mountain to the North,
a Lake to the South,
Paths to the West,
a River to the East

far away from here, and from the viewpoint of that faraway place this tiny district was of no interest, whoever had been here had left, everyone, to the last man, gone, not even a stray child or a noodle seller remained, no head suddenly pulled back from motionless watching behind a window grating, as one might have expected around here on a sunny, peaceful late afternoon, he established that he was alone; and he turned to the left, then he went straight on again, then he suddenly noticed that for a while the ground had been rising, the streets on which he walked, whether heading to the left or straight, had, for a while, been unequivocally leading upward, he could not establish anything more certain than that, could not say whether the incline had begun in this or that specific spot, instead there was a kind of realization, a determined overall sense: the entirety, along with him, had been ascending for a while—he reached a long enclosure wall running to the left of him, unornamented and constructed from mud bricks assembled into bamboo framework, it was painted white, its upper edge laid with crosswise, slightly battered turquoise-blue roof tiles; the footpath ran along it for some length, and nothing happened, he couldn't see anything above the wall as it had been built too high for someone to glimpse what was on the other side, there was no window, tiny door, or even a crack-sized opening; when he reached the corner, he turned to the left and from there, for a bit longer, the path followed the wall closely until finally it came to an end, its direction cumulating in a refined bridge of light wooden construction that appeared to be floating, precisely because of its refined and light character; it was covered by a roof constructed of cypress bark, its columns made of cypress wood, burnished to perfection and supporting the soft, rain-battered flooring that swayed gently when stepped upon, and on either side: there were depths, and everything was green. Down below, the small valley was overgrown with vegetation, and on all of its inclines there were luxuriantly foliaged trees, fresh maple and oak, and dense wild bushes, before him and below him and after the exit of the wooden bridge: tumultuous green, and green everywhere.

Arching across the valley, the wooden bridge came to an end, and yet nothing else began, the wall simply continued, unornamented, painted white, constructed from thick, dense mud bricks, and above, at its top, two rows of turquoise roof tiles laid against each other; he went on, persevering, looking for an entrance, and all the while he had the sense that the unyielding insularity and immutability of this wall running along to his left not only served to signal the presence of an enormous plot of land, but to inform him: this was no mere wall, but the inner dimension of something, which merely intended, with this evocation, to alert the one arriving that very soon other units of measurement would be required than the ones to which he'd been accustomed; other ratios than the ones hitherto enclosing his life would now be determinative.

III

He did not find the gate where he thought he would, by the time he noticed that he was about to step inside he was already inside, he couldn't perceive how he'd stepped across, suddenly he was just there, and facing him—he was on the other side of the wall—was the enormous gate construction known as Nandaimon: in the middle of the courtyard there suddenly rose four pairs of wide, colossal smooth-burnished hinoki columns upon raised stone plinths, and atop them a gently arching doubled roof construction; two roofs placed one above the other as if there had been a moment in which, at its beginning and its end, two enormous autumn leaves, slightly singed at the edges, were descending, one after the other, and only one of them had arrived, but truly had arrived, and now it rested on the timberwork of the columns while the other was as if still descending through the perfect symmetry of the air, which, with the unspeakably great strength of a scarcely perceptible attraction did not allow it to complete its movement, to rest upon its mate, and so it was held above, while the lower roof, already placed upon the columns, was below; two roofs, placed one above the other with hair's-breadth accuracy in the flawless harmony of the complicated brackets, and below were the four pairs of enormous columns, burnished to perfection, and the whole thing stood there with no explanation, because at first: what kind of gate was this, surrounded in every direction by a wide and empty courtyard so that accordingly one could walk around it as if it were a building, which, as it happened, was meant to be built in the middle of this wide and empty courtyard, and so it was built—what kind of gate was this, standing as high as it possibly could in the middle of a clear, square, silent plot of land; to look at its form, it was most emphatically a gate, its placement, however, remained a mystery: this gate did not betray its purpose, as if something had gotten lost, either within the gate or in the pair of eyes that looked at it, although the thought that formerly operated in the design of this gate was evidently so disciplined that only a few moments were necessary for it to become clear: this monumental structure was a gate, but a different kind of gate, one which awaited the person who arrived from a different direction and led him in a different direction, from somewhere else to somewhere else — as it stood completely alone in the empty courtyard, four pairs of enormous columns, and between them three pairs of heavy gate wings—originally it had been judged that they should be closed shut almost eternally—below an enormous arched double roof construction, slightly curving upward at its corners, lowered onto the columns—a gate in which there were, between the columns, three openings, three closed-off potential routes formerly ordered and hung there, three pairs of heavy gate wings of which the far-right leaf was smashed in: one of the wings of the gate, half broken-off, hung down from the bronze hinges, it dangled, toppled over, sagging, dead.

V

There was, of course, something labyrinth-like in the way the narrow, short streets continually ran into each other, one would set off, but a few buildings later the street had already come to an end and there was a corner where one had to turn, and then, to the left or right, there was another small street just as narrow and short as the previous, altogether a few small houses facing each other, and then that street had already come to an end, running into another, it was something like a labyrinth, of course, but at the same time the chaos causing the oscillation of the layout of these streets wasn't frightening and even less so futile, but playful, and just as there were finely wrought fences, the grated rolling gates protected by their small eaves, above, leaning out from both sides here and there, were the fresh green of bamboo or the ethereal, silver foliage of a Himalayan pine with its firework-like leaves unfolding; they bent closely over the passerby as if in a mirror, as if they were protecting him, guarding him and receiving him as a guest within these tightly closed fences and gates, these bamboo branches and the Himalayan pine foliage; namely, they quickly gave notice to the one arriving that he had been placed in safety: here he would come to no harm, here no trouble could reach him, here, he should just continue to walk peacefully among the small houses, enjoying the branches of the bamboo tree leaning out or the ethereal foliage of the Himalayan pines, he should just keep on strolling peacefully uphill, resting his gaze on the breathtaking clusters of magnolia bloom which had just now opened, enormous chalices in a plenitude of luminous white beauty, on the bare branches of this or that magnolia tree, he should just allow his attention to be distracted from the reason he had come here so that his thoughts would be diverted by the buds nearly exploding on the plum tree branches reaching out here and there from the tiny front gardens.

VI

In the distance, the Keihan line railcar in which the grandson of Prince Genji was traveling could not be seen, although there was less than a minute left until arrival. No one was waiting on the station platform, no railway employee came out from the building's service room, the employee was huddled inside, monitoring the electronic display indicating the routes of the scheduled trains, he noted down in his service notebook what had to be noted down, there was no one out there on the platform, only a mild breeze which at times swept along in front of the station building, clearing everything away in the last moment so that not even a tiny strand of hair or a fallen crumb of tobacco remained, blowing along the platform pavement and clearing everything from the route of the person whose feet would be making contact with this platform pavement, altogether there was this occasional breeze, nothing else, the occasional breeze and the inviting, winking buttons of two dilapidated vending machines, placed closely together, or rather abandoned together by the corner of the building on the right-hand side, they blinked invitingly: drink hot or iced tea, drink hot or cold chocolate, drink hot seaweed soup or ice-cold miso, the red blinking meant, on one of the machines, hot, and the blue blinking meant, on the other one, cold, it was possible to choose, press a button, and drink, the blinking buttons on the vending machine signaled—then the breeze, completely lukewarm, soft and velvety, so that everything would be as clean as possible when he got off the train.

middle, sighing in the gentle wind; this was the ginkgo, bearing within itself the numbed depths of innumerable geochronological ages, its thick trunk only able to bear a Shinto rope with its paper streamers, and below, the wild proliferation of a holly bush grown out from one of its sides; the ginkgo, accordingly, was the only one that rose from this peaceful world, and it was well visible from below as well, like a kind of tower, because everything else ended up concealing the other things, one house hiding another, one street hidden by another, only it—this colossal, and, among all the other plants, frighteningly alien and unknowable ginkgo tree—ascended, and unmistakably, as if it had arrived here directly from a hundred million years ago, the dark Cretaceous era from which it had originated, so that someone would have to notice it, someone looking up from below, from the direction of the train station, who, having arrived, and searching for the correct direction, would take a look around.

VIII

Along the Keihan line's main route, at the first stop after Shichijō no one got off and no one got on, the train stopped, the doors mechanically opened, then, after a few seconds, hissing loudly, they closed, the stationmaster held up his signal sign, then, casting a glance toward both ends of the empty platform, he pushed the button on the dispatcher's post, and finally he bowed, slowly, ceremoniously and deeply, to the empty train, as it quietly pulled out of the station to continue its journey onward: down, to the south, to Uji.

IX

A bove, on the crest of the hill, above the doubled roof of the monastery gate, there suddenly appeared, in the clear blue, luminous sky, a few enormous, dark, angry clouds, as if a menacing troop had suddenly rushed onto a mute, motionless, indifferent stage; in one moment there was still the luminous sky, and in the next—with a wind of dreadful strength at its back—this mass, coming from the northeast: gloomy, weighty, encroaching, its amplitude impossible to gauge as it kept growing, swelling into unforetold dimensions, warped, swirling, flooding, completely covering the sky within a few minutes, because a hellish tempest had driven it here, chased it, pursued it before itself, beating, shoving, thrusting forward this black lethal mass which suddenly made everything grow dark; there was silence, the birds all around grew silent, the gentle breeze died down, and then there arose a moment, and everything simply stopped: a moment during which the entire world came to a stop, and for this one single moment the murmuring of the leaves stopped, and the flexible swaying of the branches stopped; and in the conduits of the trunks and the stalks and the roots, circulation stopped, a colony of ants, which had been carrying and carrying its supplies diagonally across a path, came to a dead halt, a pebble, which had begun to roll, rolled on no further, the woodworms left off their chewing in the columns and the wooden brackets, the small rat in the vegetable garden behind the enormous cabbage paused, holding up its head, in brief every creature and plant and stone and all of the assembled secretive inner processes suddenly, for one moment, suspended all existence—so that the next moment would also arrive, and everything would continue where it had left off, the rat once again bent its head into the cabbage stump, the woodworm began chewing along its pathway again, the pebble rolled forward a little bit, but truly, everything began again: the circulation in the trunks, in the stalks and the roots, the branches' pendulums and the play of the leaves' quivering, the entire world started up again, at first just cautiously, then the birds nearby began to chirp more shrilly, above, everything above became lighter, the somber sky now clearing up from the northeast, although those weighty clouds, the dreadful tempest wind at their back, still stormed in a frenzy toward the southwest, and now nothing of that immeasurable mass even seemed credible, because only the end of it could be seen, its edge, then just a scrap, a matted, torn, ominous rag floating in the sky, which now—as if nothing had happened a moment ago—already was swimming in its former blue, the sun was shining, there was no longer any trace of that wild, tempest-like wind, moreover, in between the leaves of the gates there once again appeared that previous gentle, mild, little breeze, which began trying immediately with the leaf on the right-hand side, but of course that leaf—collapsed, broken off, its entire weight pressed against the upper bronze hinge that still supported it—had frozen into the story of its previous ruin and so remained unmovable, well, of course this breeze smoothed it up and down, chafing it a bit to see how heavy it might be, then it ran on, dashing out into the unoccupied space of the courtyard, so that, running around in a circle there, it could once again commence its particular work.

winds and high-altitude winds, there was the jet stream up there in its unattainable heights, down below was the long-awaited or dreaded ocean wind; the winds were on the mainland and they were in the caverns, they were in the axes of the river currents and they were in the autumn gardens, they were, truly in the most staggering variety possible, with their directions and dimensions, everywhere, but in reality—innumerably and unaccountably—the sum total of what occurred was that they were always here, even during lulls; and yet they were not here at all, because if they came, then nothing had come, if they left, then nothing remained of them, not even during the lulls: they were invisible when they arrived and invisible when they left, they were never able to break out of that disastrous invisibility, they existed, and yet they did not exist at all, one could know that they were here, and one could know where, it was visible as they caused the leaves on the trees to tremble, as they twisted the crown of a tree in a storm, you could see them as the dust swirled up and was chased around, in the windows slamming shut, in the litter snatched up in the street, you could hear them as they rustled and wailed and wept and whistled and howled and bellowed and grew quiet and turned into breezes, someone's face felt a breeze caressing it, or a trembling goldfinch feather on a branch fluttered, in brief, they could be seen in the world, and heard, and they could be felt there, only they were nowhere, because although everything pointed at them—movement, sound, and fragrance—it was not possible to point at them and say they existed and there they were, because their existence always proceeded in the haunting domain of the most profound indirectness, because they were palpable, but unattainable, because they were present, but ungraspable, because they were existence themselves while they themselves were excluded from existence, namely they were so close to existence that they had become identical with it, and existence can never be seen, so that, well, if they were here even when they were not here, nothing ever remained of them, only the yearning for them to come, only the fear that they would come, only the memory that they had been here, but the most painful thing of all—the grandson of Prince Genji looked up at the sky—was that the one who had once been here would never return.

XI

Behind the gate construction, at a distance measured in ken of exactly ten multiplied by two, along the courtyard's central axis, accordingly placed along the central line extending from the first gate, the Nandaimon, a second gate, known as the Chumon, stood toward the courtyard's northern end, but still cast into its wide, vacant space; it was not a mirror image of the first, nor was it simply its displacement or a mere repetition, somewhat farther back, of that first gate, but it was much more an elevation, a redoubling of its weight utilizing the same implements and on the same axis, where the sense of someone's admission, of his arrival in this space, was rendered a task, so that he who had once stepped across the high threshold of the earlier, first gate complex known as the Nandaimon now found a place of prayer, of deliverance, the disciplinary sign that from this point on, after the vile history of human existence, he would become the favored subject of such questions in a place where questions having to do with human beings no longer arose, and where the hinoki columns were made of thicker, more powerful proportions, reaching further into the heights, as, upon their complicated, vastly intricate, and wondrous system of brackets a larger, but much larger burden had to be carried than in the case of the first gate, because if on that first gate, the double roof weighing upon the columns could be said to be large, here it would be truly difficult to describe, in words, the exact dimensions of this second double-roof construction, because it was large, it was enormous, and it was colossal as it floated down from the air, and in this floating, just as with the first gate, it too remained in the air, and yet at the same time these dimensions that were larger, more enormous, more colossal, were accompanied by a nearly inexpressible weightlessness, moreover, this weightlessness, as it were, permeated every single column and brace, it permeated every element in the doubled roof construction, the dazzling rhythm of the conical clay tiles, the enchanting beauty of the roof's four corners, inclining upward, it permeated everything from the apex to the threshold; no wonder then, if, standing beneath it, the one who had arrived would feel: he was safeguarded here, he was protected, he had found refuge, because now something large was expanding above him, an appalling, formidable, glitteringly dainty wing, which was just now preparing to lift up this whole, this colossal thing—because it was almost time to lift it up.

XII

In the absence of a walkway built in the traditional sense of the kairō, the newly built wall, as if intending only to reach this far, enclosed the entire monastery grounds, confining as well the enormous square of the first courtyard, and here, placed in the center along the line of the back wall—namely, across the extended central axis of the Nandaimon and the kairō-less Chumon—set into this mud-brick wall, there was a third gate complex, much smaller and more modest than its companions: on the one hand, it was the final gate of the three, and on the other, it genuinely served as a gate, namely its task was, in the mundane sense of the word, to admit the one arriving into the successive courtyard, which was, in its formation, largely similar to the outer courtyard, comprising an unoccupied and spacious square, although in this case it was maintained in infinite tidiness; inside the courtyard, to the left, rising from the white, gravel-scattered, level ground, was a three-story pagoda with its characteristic three-winged roof construction, originally intended to house the sacred relics of the Buddha, a nobly raised wooden tower, in reality promising the Buddha's personal presence and the yearning felt for it; this pagoda, though, lacked any true entrance, any true door, it lacked any indication of even the tiniest genuine opening, there were only blind windows that looked out to nowhere and blind doors that opened to nowhere, so that, ascending, perfectly closed, to its height of three stories, it was a structure where

no one could ever step in and from where no one could ever emerge,
namely, this was truly the Buddha's house, undisturbed by human beings for a thousand years, immune to human beings for a thousand
years, he was there inside, if he was inside, a thousand years of immutability and intactness, a thousand years of air and a thousand years
of dust, a thousand years of heavy obscurity and a thousand years of
secrets, people gazing up for a thousand years in which there were a billion moments of doubt in every day and every instant as they searched,
feared, and were ashamed, comprehending nothing, stupidly; they ex-
amined and they pondered, and they wondered: if already a thousand
years had passed, then was he really still inside there, even today.

XIII

On the opposite side of the courtyard, at precisely the same height as the pagoda—although not at all in the usual place behind the Great Hall, facing both the treasure house and the sutra repository, where, generally speaking, it should have been situated — there stood a bell tower. The bronze bell, according to custom, was suspended from the inside at its center, but its weight was much greater than the dilapidated wooden construction could withstand without swaying again and again when the bell began swinging, so that, due to the highly visible lack of regular repairs, and despite the weight being centered midbeam, the entire bell tower had begun tilting a bit; the tenons of the fastening pegs discernibly no longer fit as they should, the bell ropes were frayed, the roof shingles were sliding off at one point up there, just as was clear from the bell mallet—at one time cleverly tied into a system of knotted ropes, then gradually loosening, it had fallen to the ground, left there—that there would be no one anymore to pick the mallet up, put it back in its place, and then, at the obligatory time, namely at half past four, meaning the arrival of early evening, to strike the bell with this mallet, so that, as it began to swing, the bell would reverberate throughout the monastery grounds—there would be no one because there didn't seem to be anyone here, because there seemed nothing to announce here, for a minute this section of the courtyard, with its bell tower, created that impression: no, there wasn't any need for this bell tower now, and there wouldn't be any need for it any longer, so that the first thing that would not be needed was precisely this bell tower in this abandoned, neglected section of the courtyard, as if someone were saying: let everything remain as is, let the roof shingles continue to slip down, let the ropes become even more frayed, let the pegs become even looser in the upper roof brackets, and in general: let the whole thing keel over more and more with every passing day, so that by the time the bell mallet, lying on the ground, is overgrown by weeds, the tower too will collapse, the entire one thousand years disappearing without a trace.

Only a tiny, silver-feathered, proud, short-beaked singer thought, in this moment, that it was greatly needed here: it swirled down from the heights in a sharp, playfully whimsical falling arc, perched upon the glimmering bronze ornament of the tower's peak, and picking up its little head, launched into such a rich, mellow, heartrending song in the silence of the sun-drenched late afternoon, that if there were a mate anywhere nearby it would have most certainly won its attention in the space of a single minute.

For that song lasted only a single minute. When it stopped, the little bird ascended suddenly into the sky along a straight line, then, tracing the form of a few rising and falling ellipses it was gone, ascending into the distance, so high up that there was no eye that could have been capable of discerning that tiny spot, that tiny point, like the tip of a needle growing ever smaller in the shimmering distance of the azure-blue firmament.

XIV

The stone used to form the perfect surface of the courtyards—
which, for a long time, had been designated as kogetsudai—did
not originate from the surrounding areas, but, among others, had been
originally mined from the slopes of carefully selected silicate mountains located in the pleasant area of Takasago, located approximately
a good one hundred nautical miles from here; there it was crushed
into tiny pieces by enormous millstones turned by mules and then
dispatched to Kyoto, which held the entire country under its spell,
delivered via small handcarts to the more noble monasteries, just as it
had been delivered here, to the Fukuine district, to cover the rearmost
grounds of the monastery, a somewhat neglected spot between the
agricultural buildings and the vegetable gardens, so that certain young
monks, assigned to this task, set to attaining the appropriate, unified
measurement of the crushed stones by using heavy sledgehammers,
then carried the crushed stones to the courtyards to spread them out
there; then, after a larger storm or after a heavy rain shower or simply
for the joy of greeting the spring or at dawn, toward the end of the
second month they would take the wide, thick-handled rakes and give
the stones their final form, namely on the one hand to create again
and again that perfect horizontal plane, and on the other, by using the
teeth of the rake, they drew, into the white-gravel surface, those parallel
undulations, so that there would come about not merely the idea but

the reality of the perfection of paradise which seemed to wish to evoke
the ocean's restless surface, its eddying waves here and there between
the wild cliffs, although in reality, it dreamt—into the incomparable
simplicity of that beauty—that there was everything, and yet there was
nothing, it dreamt that in the things and the processes, existing in their
inconceivable, ghastly velocity, enclosed within a seemingly intermi-
nable constraint of flashes of light and cessation, there was yet a dazzling constancy as deep as the impotency of words before an unintel-
ligible land of inaccessible beauty, something like the bleak succession
of the myriad of waves in the ocean's gigantic distance, something like
a monastery courtyard where, in the peacefulness of a surface evenly
covered with white gravel, carefully smoothed over with a rake, a very
frightened pair of eyes, a gaze fallen into mania, a shattered brain could
rest, could experience the sudden enlivening of an ancient thought
of obscure content, and at once begin to see that there was only the
whole, and no parts.

XV

The grandson of Prince Genji stood in the third gate, looking at the tower of the pagoda. The breeze once again ran across the courtyard, reaching him as well, causing the lower flaps of his kimono to flutter slightly.

His arms crossed on his chest, he did not move for a while, because he was of the opinion that one of the monks—someone he could speak to—would eventually appear. But not only was there not any sign of life of any monk, not even a servant emerged, or some attendant coming from the back, the kitchen, the bath, or the vegetable gardens, running over to him, out of breath, to be at his disposal.

Everywhere, complete silence reigned, with not a single soul in the inner courtyard, so that he—his feet slipped in their geta hardly brushing against the ground—began to walk, with slow steps, toward the Golden Hall.

In front of the entrance to the Hall, he lit incense, reverently standing to the side of the copper cauldron, he folded his hands in prayer, and bowed his head.

Then, he said within himself: May the Buddha be merciful, and grant me some light as to where I should seek.

Then he said within himself: May the Buddha be merciful, and tell me if there is any meaning at all to this seeking.

And then he said within himself: We do not know what you thought about the world. We misunderstand every one of your words. We are utterly lost.

And, to conclude, he added: Just as you once prophesied, dear, sweet, unforgettable Buddha.

The grandson of Prince Genji then lowered his hands, holding them tightly to his sides, raised his head, and bowed deeply, twice.

XVI

Down below, halfway down, another path led up to the ginkgo tree—not the one used by the grandson of Prince Genji just a short moment ago—but the ginkgo tree could be approached from the back as well, from the hill's steep incline, which, however, was inaccessible to any person as it was densely overgrown with thickets and sloped upward so precipitously. It could hardly even be called a path, instead it was a closed, narrow little track, completely concealed beneath the prickly branches and the closed, intergrown thicket leafage, rendering it invisible, and extending a kind of protection to any being that might be moving around here, and indeed a being was moving along here in this sunlit, brilliant, morning silence, a being visibly in need of the greatest protection, if the appalling manner with which it dragged itself along could be referred to as "movement": a beaten dog, half dead, now climbed up the incline, beneath the protection of the thick shrubbery and the intergrown thickets, an unfortunate dog of indeterminable breed, swimming in bloody sludge, its fur matted, weakened, emaciated to the bone, and infinitely exhausted. In reality, it had almost been half beaten to death: it could not walk on one leg, the back right leg, and so continually tried to hold it up in the air as it dragged itself forward with its three other legs, and on that same side, one of the dog's eyes was completely turned out of its socket, and its fur was bloodied everywhere, matted in clumps underneath its stomach as well as near its head which it held turned to one side as it continued its torturous route upward, as if, on the other side, it could still see something with its left eye. From its wounds, it could not be determined if the dog had almost been bludgeoned to death with a cane or had managed to escape the trap of some kind of perverse, horrific, bestial torture.

The slope was truly very steep, and this clearly was taking its toll: the dog's movements became ever slower, its stomach drooped ever closer to the earth, that stomach on which it was nearly sliding upward, as if from fear its viscera might spill out: in order to hold itself as low as possible to the ground, the dog kept bending its three more or less still functioning legs; it was losing ever more strength, ever more frequently it had to stop and lie down so that, after a few minutes, it could set off again. Its chest was heaving rapidly, vehemently, it took tiny breaths as if breathing too were painful, as if it could take ever less air into its broken-down lungs, but it was breathing, erratically and moaningly, and it didn't give up, it panted, it climbed up farther holding its back right leg in the air, its head turned to the left so that it could see in front at least a little bit, so that it might avoid the branches' prickly tips, but of course it couldn't avoid all of them, so that those branches still at times tore gashes into its skin, and then it softly whimpered, stopped and trembled, slowly lowering itself to the ground, and then set off after a few minutes once again.

It had a certain goal, and it seemed evident that whatever was making it torture itself on this steep and dangerous route was something very important; and it was evident, from its dreadful exertions, that it would reach this goal.

Its goal was the ginkgo tree.

When the dog reached the tree from the back where no one from the road could have noticed it, where neither any person or animal could have seen it, when, with its trembling limbs, it dragged itself over to the tree's thick trunk, which, on this side, was thickly covered by a young holly bush, it crawled in among the leaves so that it would become truly invisible, it squeezed its shuddering body as tightly as it could against the ginkgo's warm trunk, it released, from its tortured limbs, the remnants of its strength, it lay down, sighed one last time, then, without a single sound, within a few minutes, it silently expired.

XVII

Everything was intact, and everything appeared to be intact in the monastery. Nothing disturbed the inner silence of the kondō; from outside, the fragrant smoke of the sandalwood incense slowly snaked upward from the incense burner, lit a moment ago. The Buddha himself, chiseled at one time from a piece of expensive kashi oak no larger than the size of a small child, stood motionlessly inside, placed in a wooden box at the center of the altar, the box plentifully gilded both inside and out and signifying a special protection; in the back, the box was closed off by a thin wall; its other three sides were comprised of fine wooden trelliswork so that a certain amount of light entered into the box, meaning its inhabitant was somewhat visible, and should a believer seek out his glance, he too could gain some awareness of the world from there. He was motionless, he never changed, he had stood on that same point for a thousand years, always in his place, in the exact middle of the inordinately secure, gilded, wooden box, he stood imperturbably, always in the same robes, always frozen in the noblest of gestures, and during that one thousand years nothing had changed in the carriage of his head, in the beautiful, famous gaze: in its sadness, there was something heartbreakingly refined, something unspeakably noble, his head turned away from the world most decisively. It was said about him that he turned his head away because he was looking backward, to the back, toward a monk known as Eikan, whose speech was so beautiful, that he, the Buddha, wished to know who was speaking. The truth, however, was radically different, and whoever saw him immediately knew: the Buddha turned his beautiful gaze away so that he would not have to look, so he would not have to see, so he would not have to be aware of what was in front of himself, in the three directions—this wretched world.

the precise instructions of an infallible plan, that no one could cast into doubt, no pilgrim arriving with his mundane experience, and of course no pilgrim ever did, for surely he himself experienced that upon arriving here, approaching the Great Southern Gate, that whoever stepped across the high threshold of the Second, the Chumon gate building, then entering the inner courtyard, and glimpsing, from one direction, the three-story pagoda, and on the other side the bell tower with that bird that just now had been singing—such a pilgrim would in no way have to reflect as to what direction he should follow in this monastery, because the paths, the footpaths, marked on both sides with wooden pegs driven into the earth and lengths of twisted rice-straw rope, led the way; the pilgrim would always precisely and unmistakably find that building which should exactly follow in fostering his immersion: he would first recognize the silence of the Golden Hall, known as the kondō, and that of the teaching hall, then the courtyards and gardens following one after the other, so that he would glimpse, from the Golden Hall, the ornamental lock on the door leading to the personal domain of the abbot, as well as the visitors' premises, he would miss nothing, and he would not forget to visit even one single sanctuary, even if he felt for a long time that he was certainly going to forget something, perhaps the most essential pavilion, since the whole thing as a map, one could say, was still not present in his head, but no, not at all, the path of a visit here, built upon the suggestion of proffered spiritual immersion, was accordingly directed by whimsy, an ethereal, otherworldly whimsy, light, playful, operating with an improvisation of particular strength and yet flawless, the creation of which—this sublime monastery—might appear, in a merely superficial and rash judgment, as the impure mixture of the chaotic, of elements thrown and cobbled together, as it were a huge pile with everything thrown on top, the exigent and the slipshod, the valuable and the muddled; but no, not at all, because this whimsy was itself like the void, namely it was identical to that which had created the bright blue of the firmament above, that which had prescribed to the dog, sentenced to death, which path to follow, beneath the thorny bushes, to liberation, it was the same whimsy that wrote out the succession of the winds, the structure of the ginkgo tree's roots, the pitches and rhythm of the singer's melody on the roof of the caving-in bell tower—and that heartbreakingly refined, incomparable sadness in the averted gaze of the Buddha in the kondō.

XIX

The grandson of Prince Genji did not regain his strength. Clutching his handkerchief in his hand, for a while he hoped that someone connected with the monastery would come running over to him, but when it became clear that here outside he awaited such a person in vain, trusting that he would find someone in one of the sanctuaries, he continued his route, hurrying toward the closest one. The closest building was the teaching hall; when he reached the entrance, he slipped out of his geta, and, holding them in his hand, barefoot, or more precisely, with the traditional coverings, the tabi, on his feet, he stepped into the silent order of the sanctuary, and while he marveled at the perfect tidiness that reigned within—the cushions placed in parallel lines, the regular repetitions of the columns within the building's simple symmetry, and, placed next to the cushion of the supervising monk, the beauty of the low table, its tea bowl concealed on a shelf, the incense holder and the bamboo cylinder for storing the incense sticks next to it—he realized, with a glance of recognition, that everything, to the fullest possible measure, was in its place: the cushion of the monk leading the ceremonies, as well as, somewhat in front of him, to his right, placed with flawless precision and artlessness, the double hanging wooden beam used to strike the bell, designating the beginning and the end of meditative immersion; and the inkin, the small bronze handbell sitting on its pillow sewn from noble silk, along with the small mallet, just as there stood the two enormous chief pillars of the Buddha altar, luminous with gold and tranquility, everything was in perfect order, he realized, in a continual state of vertigo, the entire interior was immaculate with all the thoroughness one might have expected; through the paper panels of the shojis and the fusumas precisely enough light filtered in for him to be able to make his way to the sanctuary's back entrance, but as there was not a living soul there either, he could only do so much; here, in this hall, he could not remain: he could cross the room, but nothing more; in addition, as he traversed this path, the thought flashed through him that he no longer had anything to think about; he felt more and more that his strength was leaving him, he could not go on, he needed to sit down and rest somewhere as quickly as possible. He therefore stepped out of the hall, slipped back into his geta, and walked along a covered walkway toward a smaller, modest-looking lesser shrine: there he sought out the farthest, most undisturbed spot on a wooden terrace running along the length of tiny garden, raised a good meter above it, a terrace which was in fact an extension, opening onto the garden and courtyard, of the smaller shrine's inner flooring; he sat down, leaned his back against a column, wiped his sweat-covered forehead, and when, in the benevolent silence descending upon him, it struck his ear that somewhere nearby a tiny spring brook was bubbling away, he finally closed his eyes, and he thought he would sleep a bit in the midst of this peaceful tranquility—but he did not sleep, he merely lost consciousness. The blood rushed out of his pale, refined features within a moment, and his body slipped to one side of the column. His head knocked down forcefully onto the terrace flooring, and he remained there, lurched over to one side. The kimono buckled and crumpled up on his back, one of the geta fell off his foot, and only the fingers of his right hand still moved for a while, until they slowly stiffened like the muscles of the dog, beaten to death, at the base of the ginkgo tree—they opened very

decades later, but finally on one given day, the sacred ritual of tree-felling would commence, namely, first and foremost, according to the traditional order of kokoroe, ultimately including the master carpenter's vow that, with the felling of the hinoki, "no such activity would be undertaken which would lead to the cessation of the life of these trees," and they could begin cutting down the trees, pruning them, selecting, then transporting them by land and along river cascades, then, after the precise designation of tasks to be completed on-site—in this case accordingly the determination of the type and pathways of covered walkways connecting the main shrines—the timeless, simple art of the carpenter could begin: the marking and laying of foundations, securing column bases, implementing drainage ditches, the definitive, great operation of preparing the columns, cutting them down to the correct dimensions, joining them by tenon and mortise, and burnishing them to perfection, tasks which required months of labor, then bringing the structure itself to life: the elevation of the columns, joining the interconnected framework, the construction of the roof, laying down and fastening the flooring, there were hundreds and hundreds of such tasks, the mere preparation for which took months, hundreds and hundreds of such tasks, the supervision of which altogether was entrusted to a single person, the miya daiku; everyone else completed his own task, precisely, flawlessly, according to methods learned and experienced for long years ever since childhood, and finally, as the result of this cooperation, there was finally built, similar to the monastery's other shrines, a complex system of so-called covered walkways: a wondrous guider of souls, where now, in the abandonment of this ghostly desert, in this unfathomable hour of frightening silence covering the entire monastery, it was so utterly peculiar that only from here, from the direction of these covered walkways, it seemed as if a sound could yet be heard: as if, in the complete silence, a single tiny memory were now being reissued from the long flooring planks, sanded down and traversed until their surface was as smooth as glass, a memory from the history of all the steps that ever trod upon it, a history preserved for a thousand years, because precisely on the other side of the boundary of silence and yet decisively audible, the flooring creaked once in that spot precisely where its suspension was a bit more uncertain, because there, the walkway planking creaked, repeating and evoking once again the single weight of a former footstep, the certainty of a memory that someone had once tread here.

XXI

He had already put a good few streets, some tiny intersections, and corners behind himself, and from this point on it was not only his feeling but his decisive experience as well that the road was leading upward, there could no longer be any doubt that he was not merely making his way up a gentle hillock as he might have earlier hypothesized, but that he was climbing a steep slope which might have been one of the northern foothills of Mount Oishi of the Eastern Mountains. Due to the near-total development of the area, it would be incorrect to speak of any natural vegetation for a good while yet: it was only when he glanced down from the bridge, namely when he glanced below the bridge down to the gorge, that he might have realized that the characteristic vegetation here was comprised for the most part of densely growing maple and oak trees, janohige, haran, various varieties of rhododendron and podocarpus, and finally a good few Japanese larch and cypress trees. The presence of the evergreen plants, as he gazed at them, filled him with a sense of tranquility, in particular the larch trees: from their trunks and height, he judged, as he crossed the bridge, that they could be at least three or four hundred years old; with their hovering, diaphanous foliage, their straight russet trunks with the bark peeling off in thick strips, they were always very dear to him—one or two of the trees grew so tall that, emerging from the bottom of the very deep valley, their upper foliage almost brushed against, almost caressed, the one crossing the bridge. It was not possible to see farther from this point; on one side, the high monastery wall blocked the view, on the other, there was the enormous ginkgo tree; it was only when he had gone for a good while on foot alongside the wall and, reaching the proper entrance, looked around for a moment before entering, that he saw, in the distance, the Eastern Mountains with their nearer and farther peaks, although he only saw as much of them as custom and the experience of the previous thousand years would allow, namely that of course they were there all around, with their delicate tints of greens shading into blue, they naturally announced their own distance, that this mountain, upon which he now stood, also belonged to them, this mountain and its monastery was just one among them, namely, he established with the obscure, dead background of his attention, before entering the monastery grounds: there was this great whole, these so-called Eastern Mountains, and these Eastern Mountains, just as they had done during the previous thousand years, so now too wished to inform him in this moment before he stepped into the monastery located in the vicinity of the Oishi peak, that he could go ahead and proceed, he could be completely at his ease, because the Eastern Mountains, from this direction, signified unconditional protection for the enchanting city of Kyoto.

XXII

The grandson of Prince Genji did not appear to be preoccupied for a good long while with how every street and every house was completely deserted, and as, when he was first confronted with this fact, it occurred to him that there might be some kind of celebration going on somewhere or some kind of problem, he remained with this explanation and did not brood on whether it was a celebration or a problem, his attention was captured by the charming alleyways, his subtle perception of heading upward, the expectation of reaching what he had come here for, the wondrous proportions of the inner courtyards, glimpsed between the latticework of the low wooden fences, the correct placement of this or that nobly proportioned rock with the gentle foliage of a dwarf cypress leaning above it, his thoughts were occupied by the stone wells next to the gates, the gentle plashing of the water trickling onto bamboo trays, he was obliged to stop and look for a moment at this or that particular arrangement of a private garden: the perfect illusion of a dry waterfall, the thoughtful placement of a tiny pavilion, a vantage point from where the entire little garden could be observed, in brief he did not reflect upon whether, behind this complete depopulation, there was a celebration or a problem, moreover he even forgot about it, so that it didn't even occur to him when standing by the monastery entrance and glancing back for a moment at the Eastern Mountains with their delicate tints of greens shading into blue, that it was not tranquility, peace, and security they diffused in this direction, as he had thought in the obscure, dead background of his attention, but instead it was a kind of dark tension, an ominous communication, a threatening message, with which they unequivocally wished to signify, decisively wished to communicate and convey to him, to draw his attention, with their green tints shading into blue, that no—be careful, because these mountains did not signify protection to him any longer, nor to anyone, nor to the enchanting city of Kyoto, unconditionally.

XXIII

M ount Hiei, truly offering protection to the city, located at the
highest end of the Eastern Mountains, and with it, the famous
Enryaku-ji, was very far away from here; that is why the monastery had
to fulfill the ritual obligatory protective measures in their entirety on
its own, with no external support. The monastery grounds were established at the top of the mountain's southern slope, namely to the northeast, the traditional direction of danger, it was protected by the mountain peak; to the south, following the prescriptions, there was a lake,
even if—due to the unsettled forest of houses, chimneys, roofs, poles,
TV antennas, and electrical wires—it could not be seen from up here;
just as, to the east, there flowed the River Kamo, and to the west there
was the required path, moreover, as far as that was concerned, there
was more than one path leading to the monastery, and all of them exclusively emerging from the west, just as from here, the only single
route led to the west, in brief, the placement of the monastery fully
complied with the four great prescriptions: that it be protected by a
mountain to the north, a lake to the south, paths to the west, and a river
to the east—these were the four great prescriptions, so that when the
location was, in this way, perfectly designated, and the intention, dimensions, and objective of the construction of the monastery announced, the miya daiku could begin his work, and with this, a lengthy
process began which took not simply years, but decades, a process in

again and again for weeks and again for weeks on end, and he observed, circumspectly, the development of the hinoki cypress trees on the mountain that had been acquired so as to monitor them and see how they grew on the north slope and see how they grew on the south slope, to see how they were forming on the mountain peak and how they were forming at the foot of the mountain, because for the work to come they needed precise observations, he needed to know how the sun shone upon the hinoki trees in the summer, how they withstood the monsoon's long rains, and so the miya daiku lived with the trees, literally, he knew each one separately as if they were all members of one colossal family, and he proceeded in this way, truly, for years, long, long years, consequently it was not surprising if, from the very first discussion with the order's hierarchy to the mere initiation of construction an unbelievable amount of time had passed, so much time that an entire forest's worth of Japanese cypress trees had grown to a suitable age, and this was genuinely astonishing to many, and many were unduly baffled by having to wait so long, only that—as the miya daiku informed the uncomprehending—it had to be this way, and the reason why was that it could not be otherwise, namely the felling of the hinoki cypress trees could come to pass only and exclusively at the appropriate time, and as to what the appropriate time was, he, only and exclusively he, the master, knew, and he knew this from his own ancestors, and he even said that he knew when, and he did not hesitate to announce when this so-called appropriate time had come, and he could ask the abbot for the sign for holding the kokoroe ceremony, and the ceremony could be held, and in the first hour of felling the trees he could make a vow in which he, the miya daiku, had to promise, standing before the first hinoki tree, that he, with his own life, assumed responsibility for not squandering the life of the hinoki tree, but that "he would grant it the life of beauty," and only then could the real work begin, and the grumblers began to understand that those years and those decades had been

50

truly necessary, nicely and slowly they began to understand everything when they saw, and when it was explained to them, that from among the Japanese cypress trees that were felled, transported, and then immersed in the River Kamo for the period of one full year, the heavy columns, supporting a substantial weight, the framework of the sanctuaries, would be fashioned from those trees that had grown on the mountain peak; the base of the mountain provided the timber for the long lintels, because the trees at the mountain's base had to struggle more intensely to reach the sunlight than the trees on the mountain peak, and as a consequence the trunks of the trees from the mountain's base were more attenuated, longer and thinner than the trunks of the trees on the mountain peak, which were, however, thicker and stronger, and so on, and then it was not too difficult to see that in the course of the previous decades everything had been proceeding according to a well-thought-out and monumental plan, guided by the wise counsel of ancient experience according to which every aspect of the construction of the sanctuaries must reflect, with hair's-breadth precision, the natural life of the trees on the mountain in Yoshino, namely the trees that had grown on the northern slope of the mountain in every case were used for the northern walls of the shrines; the roof timber of the shrines was exclusively comprised of cypress wood that had originally grown on the mountain peak in Yoshino, namely in the end it became perfectly clear to everyone that each individual hinoki cypress tree was granted exactly that place in each sanctuary building that it had occupied during its natural life on the mountain, and that each individual tree, within its own lifespan, took its place among the columns, the entablature of the bracket beams, or the roof vaulting to the extent that its own internal structure made it mature for this particular task, namely they had to withstand the cruel blows of time, the miya daiku explained on one occasion to his young disciple, they had to withstand time, he explained to him, when they stood, just the two of them, at golden sheets—it was, in brief, at the same time as the construction of the halls, the rooms, the cells, and the pavilions, the covered walkways, the breathtaking roof structures, the pagoda and bell tower, the triple gate system, as well as the outer enclosure wall, that the carving of the statues for later placement in the shrines also took place: the sacred operations were commenced, so that after a while the odd situation emerged that in the workshops—which otherwise were not located on the building site but in the city, on the other side, as they had migrated to the proximity of the western mountains—the enormous Buddhas and Bodhisattvas had stood completed for a while now, ready to be taken to their definitive places in the monastery sanctuaries; they had to wait, though, for decades, or in the case of this or that extraordinarily important Buddha statue, when construction was taking a very long time, they had to wait years in the workshops' protected storerooms, so that their removal to their definitive places could finally ensue, because of course the monastery took longer to complete than the statues, so that for a long time still, certain privileged monks and illustrious persons went to admire them, people to whom such viewings were permitted, and they did admire them as befitting their merit, for truly every statue was captivatingly beautiful, from the enormous Amida Buddhas, each one seated on his colossal lotus throne, immersed in infinite tranquility, to the depictions of the inimitably peaceful Shakyamuni, to the smallest Buddhist protector deities— only that no one knew, because no one had any idea, neither the most initiated or the most privileged, no one knew where the Buddha statue, ordered for placement in the center of the Golden Hall and intended as the chief guardian deity for the entire monastery, no one knew where, in which workshop it was, nor who had carved this most important of Buddhist statues or who was carving it right now, because this was kept in the greatest of secrecy, no one could know anything about this, no one could see this, moreover the entire thing was organized so that

54

the head monks of the order kept deliberately mixing up the various bits of information they disseminated in order to confuse the curious seekers, so that several believed that they, but only and exclusively they, were informed as to where, in which workshop, and who was carving the Buddha statue, and finally there were quite a few who believed that they, and only they themselves, were the keepers of this secret, those who were convinced that they and only they knew where the famous Buddha was being prepared, the rumors and the hearsay spread, but in reality almost no one knew anything entirely up till the day when the monastery was consecrated, and the Buddha, his head turned to one side in his gilded box, finally ended up in his place—so that the exact opposite of what everyone had been expecting occurred, because no, during the celebration of the consecration ceremonies, from the high-ranking believers to the ordinary onlookers, it was not signs of wonder and prostration, not emotion and gratitude that people displayed, now that they saw that, finally, after long decades, the main deity had taken up his place in the monastery, instead it was shock, because in reality everyone was shocked, everyone who passed before the Buddha to wonder, to make an offering, moreover, even the simplest souls were directly frightened by what they glimpsed, amid the great pushing and jostling in the place of honor of the Golden Hall.

Because this Buddha was small, as small as a three-year-old child—this Buddha was thin and frail, seeming more as if he were in need of protection—he did not sit enthroned upon the lotus, but instead stood in a gilded box like someone who was here just for a moment, and that noble, otherworldly sadness in his gaze and the way he turned his head away prophesied such a whirlwind of scandal that the leaders of the order, during the week immediately following the consecration ceremonies, decided they would look for that document—even if it didn't exist—from which the sequence of events could be clearly elucidated: namely that Eikan, that wondrous speaker of old, spoke, and the Buddha was so charmed by the strength of his beautiful words that he looked around to see who it was, and he remained there, eternally, bearing witness to how the beauty of the human word, if accompanied by truth, was irrevocable, and so on, and so on, and in this way, they would cleverly reverse the disadvantage of being heavily burdened with unforeseen consequences into an advantage, and thanks to its happy diffusion, the whirlwind of scandal died down even before it could have begun swirling up, and so he, the frail Buddha of unparalleled beauty could receive the false wonder and the false offerings for one thousand years, foreshadowing his future fate, as after a while, they would move him from one shrine to the next, because he would not find his place, they would try to propagate the legend with this Eikan or someone else, but they couldn't, because that head, turned to one side, would speak plainly of the unsalvageable story of baseness, because that head, turned to one side, would speak eternally of beauty, of motionless evil and impotent nobility, of incurable indifference and exaltedness moldering away at even the slightest hint of human presence, of inextirpable stupidity and ineffectual sympathy—and all this protected by merely a small gilded box, with its thin wooden lattice on three sides, with a wall, butterfly-thin, to the back, in the center of the altar in the Golden Hall.

XXV

A swallow flitted across the terrace, and perhaps this gentle contact—as a completely gentle descent and a completely gentle
ascent, compressed into two moments, slightly agitated the air with
its abrupt, silent momentum—was the reason that the grandson of
Prince Genji once again regained consciousness. He didn't know how
much time had passed; from the angle of the sunlight he concluded
that it must be afternoon already. He noticed the handkerchief fallen
in the garden's dust, he leaned down from the terrace to retrieve it, he
picked it up and brushed it off, then, collecting his geta, pulled them
onto his feet, squeezed the handkerchief in his hand, and set off along
the length of the lesser shrine. He supported himself at times against
the columns or, losing his balance, involuntarily reached out for the
shoji frame by the pavilion wall, stepping forward haphazardly, he
could not think, his head was aching, and clearly he had no idea where
he was going.

He was staggering considerably, he couldn't see clearly, at every step
he had to grab onto something.

He reached a closed courtyard surrounded by a stone wall, passing
before some kind of stone steps with only a couple of risers which led
to a simple gate similarly carved from stone, he walked in front of this
entrance and cast a glance in that direction to see what was inside—
that, too, was a kind of courtyard, some kind of garden, perhaps with a

little house, a completely tiny little house, as if there, toward the back of the garden, there were also a small wooden shrine, although it looked more like an unimpressive hut, used only by the person who resided there, or perhaps not even by him too much; he glanced for a moment at the pair of stone steps, he saw the stone vaulting in a flash, and he saw what was there inside, a garden that seemed fairly unimpressive, moreover somehow abandoned, moreover absolutely neglected, and already he was moving forward, after a few steps he had forgotten all about it, for him it simply had no significance whatsoever, to speak the truth: he didn't even notice, didn't even grasp that he had seen something, it was only his blind vision that sensed just now: there had been something, although something of no interest, and so he went on, proceeding fairly quickly given the intermittent shakiness of his legs, sometimes he stopped, leaning with one hand on something, whatever happened to be nearby, most often a wall, because at this point there seemed to be a wall made of simple crude stone beside him, then he continued onward, but it was clear that he himself didn't know where he was going or why he was going there, and mainly what the purpose of this going on was when he was overcome by such a persistent weakness, because, truly, now he was very weak, weaker than he'd ever been before, because now he really had to lie down somewhere and drink, a glass of clean water, at last, because he was dizzy, so dizzy that he could hardly even see where he was walking.

XXVI

Generally speaking, the sacred sutras of a given order's temple were always kept in a distinguished place, most frequently the back section of the main altar of the Golden Hall, in cabinets of fine workmanship burnished to a fine surface, finely varnished and well-guarded by locks, and here too this is what occurred, here too, those sutras, which, were among the most important, most valuable, and most ancient, bearing particular ritual significance, were guarded in locked cabinets built into the wall behind the altar; although, diverging somewhat from general later custom, in this monastery the most ancient of traditions was followed, namely two separate buildings were built for all the other sutras and books, two buildings of identical dimension, thoroughly congruous in their form, roof structures, beam work, every aspect of their outer form, they stood behind the Golden Hall to the right-hand side of the next courtyard, and the first building, the shōsō, was dedicated to the storage of the order's greatest treasures, and the second, the kyōzō, standing approximately twenty hiro, that is to say approximately twenty fathoms from the shōsō, was reserved for the storage of sutras for daily use, as well as for all other bibliographic masterworks. These two halls—facing, at something of a distance, the complex of buildings where normally, following the order's traditions, the bell tower would be built at the other end of the courtyard, although here instead were monks' cells, guesthouses, and offices—these halls did not resemble the other buildings of the monastery in any way, they were not connected with any other pavilion, they were not joined into the system of covered walkways, their dimensions were different, their floor plans were different, they stood on enormous, colossal hinoki columns, namely, they were raised, and in this way, the buildings themselves commenced approximately at a height of one-and-a-half ken above the tamped-down earth, and the span between the columns had not been filled with anything, namely their "raising" was well visible; in addition, the buildings' walls were not constructed from bamboo trellis and plastered in mud mixed with chaff, but were instead assembled from straight hinoki beams, somewhat roughly worked, and horizontally fastened to each other with the simplest cross-joining technique possible, in addition to which, in singular fashion, both buildings were surrounded by a thin, simple, airy, almost rustic plank fence, and, if the same tiles as elsewhere were used here on the roofs, both the treasury and the sutra repository wished to signal, in the most decisive way possible, that their meaning, purpose, mission, and ritual significance were different from that of every other shrine on the monastery grounds, and they did express this, first and foremost in that neither of them had any windows: the four walls of each building were comprised of horizontal hinoki beams, regularly and continuously stacked and perfectly closed, and comprised of nothing else, accordingly both buildings were nearly completely walled-in structures—almost completely closed, because exactly in the middle of each main facade, there was a door opening with two heavy leaves, so there was, naturally, an entrance, namely exactly in the middle of each building, altogether two doors, two entrances, four heavy leaves carpentered from akamatsu wood, the two uniform buildings were based on the same principles, located approximately twenty hiro, that is to say twenty fathoms from each other—only that the state of repair of each was completely different; their condition was not even comparable.

The treasury had been set on fire, but in an inconceivable way, as if the goal hadn't been robbery, namely on the building no other marks of damage at all were visible: even the expression "set on fire" seemed a little exaggerated, as the intent to set the structure on fire was only visible on the upper beams and roofing, as they had lost their colors, and here they were, orphaned and soot-blackened atop the singed hinoki columns—but no one had opened the door, it appeared that no one had even tried to break in: the door leaves were unscathed, the lock appeared to be intact, not even a scratch anywhere or even the slightest trace of an attempted forced opening, no, nothing, in contrast to the building housing the sutra repository, which had not been set on fire, but—in some distant, inexplicable, and perhaps not completely inadvertent parallel with the ruined gate of the Nandaimon in the first courtyard — both of the door leaves were damaged and broken; here as well they had only been able to tear off the leaves from the hinges in the lower corners, the upper hinges were somehow still holding up the doors to a certain degree, so that they hung down like the sad memory of their own task; and through the opening that had arisen, light filtered into that place where previously no one had ever been granted admission.

The sutra repository had been planned to remain in darkness; in it, the books would be protected.

The grandson of Prince Genji slowly walked around the four walls of the shōsō, then he stood in front of the second repository.

He looked at the broken door.

At last, there was someplace for him to enter.

Perhaps he would find a glass of water inside.

He took off his geta, carefully placing them at the foot of the steps, then, in his white tabi, he went up the stairs with noiseless footsteps, and carefully raising his leg across the high threshold, he stepped into the shrine.

XXVII

The cutting of the bamboo strips demanded extraordinary care. Great attention had to be paid to the humidity of the seasons, as well as all of the circumstances involved in the process of drying the bamboo leaves cut into thin strips, and of such circumstances there were always plenty: one had to be familiar with the assembled properties of the given type of bamboo, beginning with its sensitivity at different times of year, among different climatic conditions, one had to know how it behaved both in warm weather and in cool shadow, in dull or in sharp sunlight, one had to observe simply everything in the entire world, so that the bamboo strips, first cut, then rubbed with an antipest preparation, and carefully dried above fire would truly be suitable for their purpose, namely so that their surface would be smooth and even, and so that after the attainment of this beauty and smoothness it would be possible to write upon these bamboo strips, because this was the idea, the first sutra texts were, in the beginning, written on such strips of bamboo with brush and ink with a sure hand in tiny workshops with poor lighting, written on thin bamboo strips, their length in direct proportion to their importance; then, in a truly inventive, but somewhat complicated manner, they were attached to each other with silken strings or leather straps, so that in this way the first bamboo books were created, and these were the earliest ones, and these were not kept here in the sutra repository, but among the most precious items inside the back cabinet of the main altar of the Golden

Hall, as were the so-called wood-board books, invented at around the same time, and which should be understood as particular bibliographic masterpieces: cut into the form of a square or rectangle, their surfaces circumspectly polished, these were used for setting down missives of shorter length or announcements, namely texts not exceeding one hundred characters in length, and covered with wooden sheets of the same size, the name of both author and addressee featured on the cover board of these unparalleled masterworks, and the recipient's address, as well, of course, and finally the entire thing, namely the two wooden sheets, would be tied together with twine, knotted up, and this knot was immersed in clay, and into this the seal, with its so-called seal-head, was pressed so that no unauthorized individual could touch this letter without there being clear evidence of the breach—namely, there were things to safeguard in the cabinet behind the altar, just as in the kyōzō, too, because well, of course not only were the sutras meant for daily use kept here, but every other volume which did not need to be uncon-ditionally and directly kept in the protective proximity of the Buddha in the Golden Hall, as, for example, the silk books, kept here as well, as there was no doubt as to either the antiquity of their provenance or their value, and in the setting of the light-impoverished kyōzō, or rather due to the lesser amount of humidity, they could be maintained in better conditions than in the more open and therefore more weather-exposed interior of the Golden Hall, and so the books made of silk, ac-cordingly, these exemplars of the next great chapter in the art of book-making — because this was the next step in the creation of the book, when, namely, instead of the previously used bamboo or wood-board books, the texts of the sacred sutras began to be written upon snow-white silk, which, shortly after its discovery and diffusion, was woven expressly for this purpose in such a way that the length of the text to be written down was determined, the appropriately sized piece of silk cut, the lines serving to separate the columns of written characters wo-ven into the material itself, and the sacred texts themselves written in

for which natural means, namely sunlight, were used: the consensus was that the astounding quality of the washi paper created was to be credited exclusively to this strict discipline; in the case of the most exceptional papers, these qualities became evident only centuries later, although at that point they were very evident.

Because this, the discovery of paper, was truly the most crucial phase in the history of the book: learning how to make paper in the unparalleled workshops of China—large, astonishing in every aspect, unsurpassable and enjoying unassailable prestige—then the introduction of these techniques at home in the back crannies of monasteries and distinguished private homes, the appearance of paper and the scroll in history, first as the scroll-book, which in the beginning was prepared by pasting one end of a fully inscribed piece of paper with a strip to the next piece of paper, and that piece of paper to the next, and so on, until a long piece of paper was formed containing the entire text—which, in the beginning, was merely folded in the famous concertina formation, and this was known as sutra binding—but later on they came upon a method that ensured greater protection, namely if the paper were rolled up and stored in scroll form—at first just like that, simply, taking the paper and rolling it up, and then, on the basis of daily experience, the variation of the scroll attached to a dowel quickly came about, and with that the true scroll-book came into being in which the dowel was most often a thick piece of larch wood, finely burnished and painted; for more valuable scrolls, ivory was used, glazed clay, gold, even jade, the main thing was that the inscribed paper was wound around it, but of course how it was wound was also essential, namely the noble character of the entire thing, it goes without saying, carried extraordinary significance, just as the protective measures did, in the interest of which the written paper was mounted on silk or another kind of strong paper so as to make it more resistant and durable, and as the reinforcing silk or paper was longer than the wound scroll with the text itself, this gave the classical scroll-book its characteristic format with an additional minor detail serving both as an important practical goal and the unbounded object of the expression of yearning for beauty, namely there was also threaded into the middle of this protective cover that was longer than the scroll and wound around it, a small piece of fine twine, in this way binding the scroll onto the dowel, and for centuries the creators of these scrolls toyed with whether more decisive significance should be attributed, in the fine workmanship of this small piece of twine, to the colors, the fabric, nearly as valuable as gold, or the playful elegance of the binding itself.

XXIX

Under normal circumstances there was no chance that there inside, in the kyōzō, he would find water, he longed, rather than truly hoped for it, so he was quite surprised, when, as he entered the sutra repository, he noticed, through the light filtering in, by the entrance-way, first on the left-hand side, ten or fifteen small oil lamps placed in a wooden chest, and on the other side, to the right, a simple table and chair, as if the monk whose task it was to watch over the repository had left them; on this table was a half-filled jug of water, with two dented tin cups next to it.

He poured a few sips of water into one of the cups, at first moisten-ing his lips, then he drank it up.

Along the entire eastern wall of the repository, the tall, varnished shelves were all occupied by the monastery's scroll-books, wrapped in expensive silk with their ornamental dowels pointing outward; on a tiny wooden panel, dangling from the end of each dowel, the scroll's essential information was recorded: the author's name, the title of the sacred book, the number of the particular scroll in relation to the en-tire work, namely which sutra, which imperial message, which edify-ing religious history was bound in its material. On the western side of the kyōzō were rows of printed books, the first carved wooden-block printed exemplars, thus representing the more recent fateful chapter in the historical development of the book; one section of the shelves held

those books which had been prepared with so-called butterfly binding, where, because of the older method of stitching, two blank pages
followed two printed pages; in the other section, books were placed
in which the binding ran along the other edge of the page: the butterfly did not fly further on, the butterfly wings remained stuck inside,
because now the blank pages faced inward, where accordingly, every
page that could be folded out could now be read, and in this section,
the individual booklet-like volumes were gathered between firmer protective covers. Each work, whether a volume of the Shōshinge wasan,
containing Japanese hymns, an edition of the Kannon reigenki, the
famous poetic anthology, the Hyakunin-isshu, or a valuable Genji Mo-
nogatari Emaki, would be comprised of many thin pamphlets, so that
after a while, the usage of cardboard boxes, covered with blue fabric,
became widespread, and so it remained: from the moment of its inven-
tion, the numerous artifacts in the history of the printed book were
preserved most frequently in such boxes, as was the case here, too,
in this kyōzō where the shelves, on this side, were nearly exclusively
occupied by the large, blue, fabric-covered cardboard boxes to ensure
the safeguarding of such vulnerable pamphlets, and so the well-known
form of the traditional Japanese book came into being, strictly following, from its beginnings until the final technical developments, every
single prescription demanded by tradition, in the strictest sense of the
word, because a work could appear in any period of history, but tradition—whether it meant the significance, enduring until the end, of the
fold lines on each side of the woodblock-printed page, the so-called
"heart of the printing block," the designation and fabrication method
of the book's "mouth" and "root," the book cover corners with their
golden brocade, the variegated binding practices and materials, or, finally, the order of placement of the volumes on the lacquered shelves
of a repository, as here, for example, in the sutra repository known
as the kyōzō, located in the courtyard behind the Golden Hall, next

XXX

Someone thought they'd seen him at the first stop after Shichijō, and so that was where the eight or ten men sent to look for him got off the train on the Keihan line.

They were all wearing European clothes, and they were all thoroughly hammered.

For a good long while, behind the station, they stood, lost, tottering, perplexed, gazing at the streets that led from there. Then one of them pointed somewhere randomly, and they finally set off in that direction. The two in front clutched at each other as they led the troupe. The others followed, dizzy, reeling, stumbling. At times someone in the back yelled out to the one in front, but received no reply.

There was not a single living soul on the street, only a bit higher up, through the gate of one house opened to a mere crack, an old lady leaned out, her head leaning forward, her gaze dubious as she tried to size up who these people might be. Her suspicious expression did not auger anything good, but they had no other choice but to ask her.

Had she seen Prince Genji's grandson around here anywhere?

The old woman remained stock-still for a moment, looking them up and down as if she'd seen some kind of repulsive sludge on the sidewalk.

Then, without a word, she shook her head, and, like someone who was afraid these men might attack, withdrew into her courtyard, latched the wooden bolt on the gate, but they heard no steps indicating she was fleeing back into the house, so presumably the old woman was standing there behind the bolted gate, waiting and listening for them to be gone already.

The grandson of Prince Genji.

Drunken pigs.

She had never heard this name.

XXXI

In the inner space of the kyōzō, exactly in the middle of the shrine, a smaller replica of the kyōzō had been built. Faithful to its quadratic floor outline, but a good few shaku smaller in dimension, it followed the ground plan of the kyōzō: its four walls, comprised of shelves that were imitations of the kyōzō's interior walls, as well as the emblematic roof construction installed atop these four walls of shelves, imparted a distinguished significance to this unparalleled inner shrine; its entrance, a very narrow and low opening cut into the wall of shelves, faced the door of the kyōzō; and no secret was made of the fact that this opening was meant for only a single person, as its builders had been thinking only of one single person, who, bending his head quite low, and only by turning his body to one side, could slip into this inner space; it was envisioned that inside, in this smaller sanctuary, within the larger sanctuary, in the center of which altogether there was a single wide and low table, only one single person would sit: only one single person would, holding an oil lamp and with bent head, unfold and leaf through the pages of an opened book or unwind a scroll taken from its place of storage on either the east or the west wall of shelves, because there was simply not room for more than one person within, as the measurements of this inner shrine had been tailored so that it would be clear that no more than one person at one time would ever be expected here, that was how it was planned and that was how it was built;

and as for the task of the four walls built out of shelves, one section of which lay on the floor, knocked down and incomprehensibly smashed up, that too seemed fairly unequivocal, namely the texts indispensable to the monastery were stored on these shelves, sutras intended for daily use, more than a few good precious exemplars of which were now crushed and buried beneath the knocked-down shelf, the books lying scattered everywhere on the shrine floor, accordingly—until this break-in—several hundred identical copies of the Diamond Sutra had been preserved here, all of them with the fronts of the cardboard storage boxes bearing the works' titles, designations, and notations turned outward, so they could easily be identified from the outside, removed from the shelf, and carried out of the kyōzō without ever having to step into the space of the inner shrine which had been intended for another goal, another task, intended so that someone could immerse himself in the prayers of the Hyakumantō Dharani, so that someone seeking out the memories of the genius of Kobo Daishi could study, undisturbed, the written world of Shingon Buddhism, so that he could simply find tranquility in the unparalleled collection of the sacred books of the Tendai, the Miroku, and the Dainichi, at least a few hours of peace and seclusion—as was occurring with the grandson of Prince Genji now as well, for he truly had found this peace and this seclusion here, because avoiding the locus of destruction, he slipped through the door opening into this inner shrine and reverently bowed to the capital facing him, lowered himself down onto the tatami, then—while slowly beginning to examine, from one row to the next, the titles of the sutras that were near to him—his eyelids grew heavy, and he immediately fell into a deep sleep.

XXXII

He had read about it for the first time in the last decade of the Tokugawa, when a copy of the renowned illustrated work *One Hundred Beautiful Gardens* turned up accidentally in his hands, he leafed through it, immediately enchanted, and although all of the ninety-nine gardens were of extraordinary interest, it was the one hundredth garden, the so-called hidden garden, that captivated him, he read the description, he looked at the drawing, and the description and the drawing both immediately made the garden real in his imagination, and from that point onward he was never free of it ever again, from that point onward this hidden garden never let him go, he simply could not chase it from his mind, he continually saw the garden in his mind's eye without being able to touch its existence, he saw the garden, and after a while, self-evidently, he wanted to see it in reality as well, namely he gave out the mandate for the garden to be found, he gave the command for the search to begin without delay, only that even in the earliest phases this search encountered a fair amount of difficulty, and, well, just as the entire thing ended up later on too, it proceeded with cumbersome, agonizing slowness; continually there was just vacillation, conjecture, assumptions, the academics entrusted with this mission were perplexed, clearly trying to avoid any occasion where they would have to give any account of their progress, the halting words were all too conspicuous, whenever, at last, some famous scholar could be imposed upon to issue a statement: yes, he cleared his throat, indeed, and at the price of truly great difficulties, they had nonetheless come across a so-called trace which did appear as if it might lead somewhere, at which he, the grandson of the prince, immediately realized: there was no point to any of this, nothing of the sort had happened, they hadn't found anything, there was no trace of anything, and of course he himself was quite aware that the real reason for this was the work itself, the *One Hundred Beautiful Gardens*: from the description that could be read there, and the captivating drawing, no precise details—in a brutally playful way—were forthcoming, moreover, to admit the truth: there was no information whatsoever as to where, exactly, this concealed, seemingly truly captivating garden was located, because the city, the locality, the prefecture were all extraordinarily difficult to identify, if not precisely impossible to identify, because certainly it appeared, and more than once, that this entire enterprise was hopeless and hopeless and hopeless, that since the very beginning of the beginning this entire thing had been nothing more than a hopeless endeavor—perhaps this garden existed only in the imagination of the author of *One Hundred Beautiful Gardens*, created only as his own personal, confidential, misleading joke, and so it frequently occurred that the entire search would be simply abandoned, moreover, not even waiting for the grandson of the prince to initiate the end of the matter, individual learned dignitaries, particularly at the beginning of the Meiji era, more than once tried gathering up their courage in order to convince him to put a stop to this inquiry lasting centuries, but of course in the end there was neither courage nor deed; in great confusion, and delaying the mere report for a good long while, when the time came for it, they told him: just at that moment their search was not bringing fruition, they still hadn't found it, moreover, the work itself, *One Hundred Beautiful Gardens*, that single exemplar which was truly the most precious possession of the grandson of Prince Genji, they brought him the news on a sad day, was not in its spot in the prince's library where it was usually kept and where it should have been, it was nowhere where it could have been, even though they had turned everything upside down looking for it, even though they beheaded everyone who might have been responsible for its loss, the book had disappeared without a trace, they flung themselves onto the ground before him, it's gone, they confessed, and this garden, if it even ever existed, they said, weeping from fear of retribution, was also gone—*if it had even ever existed*, this phrase echoed in the mind of the grandson of Prince Genji, it echoed in his memory many times afterward with ever more frequency, although never with that kind of incredulous sorrow hovering in the background as among the members of his whispering retinue filled with anxiety for him; instead, from his memory's more shadowy side came a mild, persistent, forceful encouragement: well, of course it existed, of course, this garden—if the book was really lost—still really existed somewhere, undoubtedly it was very well hidden, but it was somewhere, every spring it burst into new life, every winter it returned to tranquility, a tiny little garden, as the original description had it, located in an unremarkable section of a large monastery that was never sought out by anyone, never visited, moreover abandoned, it was, however, *there*, the author of the volume announced emphatically, and whoever found this garden, he continued euphorically, whoever glimpsed it would never judge his enthusiasm, meaning the enthusiasm of the author of *One Hundred Beautiful Gardens*, as exaggerated when he wrote about this garden, because anyone who saw it would realize: this garden was the final consummation of the thought of the garden itself, this garden could be characterized, putting it most precisely, by how its creator had "attained simplicity," this was a garden—the author stated, with perceptible passion—that expressed the infinitely simple via infinitely complex forces, moreover, according to his description: an enchantment that "could not be simplified any further," an enchantment which, at the same time, radiated the full inner beauty plan, the escape, the Keihan line, and finally, walking along the side streets up the hillside.

He saw the sad pile of damaged sutras beneath the overturned shelf, he saw, in the kyōzō, the shelves to the east and the shelves to the west, he sensed the light, now almost completely that of dusk, filtering in through the broken door—when suddenly a picture flashed across his brain ... and already it had vanished, a picture, but so fleeting, that he was not even capable of establishing what it was, it had merely flitted across his brain, flung itself open and died away, and he sat there in front of the table of the inner shrine, his entire body tautened from the appearance and disappearance of the picture: it had reached him, and then left him so quickly that he could only seize its import, its weight, but from its contents nothing, so that in reality each one of his muscles was tensed, he waited for that which had unexpectedly appeared to somehow return, he forced, he tortured, he strained his memory, he forced, he tortured, he strained that damaged, overly sensitive, and ailing brain of his, if only it could call forth what it had seen, all the while knowing that it was superfluous, all the while knowing that this too was in vain, for how many times had it happened to him before that this or that scrap of memory would appear in his mind, only then to be definitively erased from there, and well, that obviously was going to happen this time as well, he established with bitterness: that picture, no matter what it had been, had vanished for good, it would never come back, as if all it were capable of was making his damaged, overly sensitive, and ailing brain flash for a mere moment, and then to erase what had flashed across it—immediately, definitively, irrevocably, forever.

XXXIII

Altogether, it only took a measure of water from the tin cup, altogether only a few hours of sleep in the tranquility of the kyōzō's inner shrine, and the grandson of Prince Genji had regained his strength.

He sat motionless in the fine fragrance of the tatami. He was exactly as motionless and exactly as wakeful now as the copies of the Diamond Sutra around him in the shelves' intact order and on the ground below, although there was nothing anymore inside that had more velocity than anything else.

It was as if he weren't even breathing. He continued to focus his gaze on the table's black varnished surface, gleaming mirrorlike, and on this gleamingly varnished table—there was nothing.

From outside, through the opening of the broken-down door, the deepening light of the sun was falling in flat planes.

Not too far behind the kyōzō, amid the dense branches of a tall azalea bush, a fox infected with rabies crouched, ready to jump.

Both of its eyes were open: it did not blink at all.

And in these numbing, motionless, troubled, crimson eyes, there was nothing else apart from burning frenzy.

Evening fell.

The magnolia trees slowly drew together their enormous petals.

XXXIV

He only moved when it had grown almost completely dark outside. He slowly got up, and with noiseless steps went out through the door of the kyōzō. He could have gone straight toward the Nandaimon as he realized he had not found what he had been looking for, he could have gone in that direction, but he decided: before he left this locale definitively, for safety's sake he would choose the other direction, and survey the entire monastery grounds.

He pulled the geta onto his feet and set off from the repository, heading downward, then he crossed to the far side of the courtyard, examining the mute facades of the management buildings, the wash-houses, the baths, and the refectory, he walked all the way to the end of the monastery, up to where the cemetery and the vegetable gardens began, where agricultural buildings had been built and fishponds installed, then he went back, walking back once again alongside the repository, the lesser shrine, and the teaching hall, he went to the far side of the courtyard and passed in front of the locked entrance of the abbot's residence, avoiding the enormous building of the Golden Hall, and finally he once again stood in front of the great bronze offering cauldron, he lit a bundle of incense thrust into the thick ashes of the cauldron, lifted his hands in prayer, and bowed his head.

***

At the end of the monastery, next to the fishponds, there stood an unassuming wooden shed. The grandson of Prince Genji had not deemed it worthy of closer examination. And in the end he was right, there was no reason why, as there was nothing there of interest to him, nothing that could have helped him.

On the side of the wooden hut, somebody had nailed up thirteen goldfish, they hung there dead, their luminous scales already withered.

The nails were driven into the wooden planks through their eyes.

XXXV

Beneath the monastery, the ground trembled.

It was a subtle trembling, quaking, tiny, hardly perceptible, but everything around here had already become inured to such things, every building had already grown so used to this sort of tremor that this time, in the monastery, it couldn't even be felt, it was perceptible both on the objects and on the living organisms that no kind of fear was flashing through them, even though it could be seen that the shrines trembled, the three large gates and the bell in its tower trembled, the brackets in the covered walkways trembled, the supporting columns, the pagoda, and all of the roofs atop the walls trembled, inside there, the Buddhas and the shojis in their frames trembled, the scrolls on the shelves and the scattered sutras on the kyōzō floor trembled, it could be seen that the dead dog outside lying at the base of the ginkgo tree trembled, and that the Buddha looking away in his gilded box trembled, but really no fear was perceptible from all of this, altogether there was merely a kind of ... waiting, somehow every single object, every single scroll, every single Buddha and every single gate and ant and magnolia and even the rat's bristles—waited, they waited to see what would happen, to see if there would be something else from this fine trembling, and that's all there was, waiting, nothing else, altogether this was what could be discerned for as long as it lasted, and the whole thing did not last longer than perhaps one single long minute, and then it was over, it stopped, came to an end, the earth calmed down, the objects calmed down, all of the shrines stopped trembling, all the gates and all the Buddhas in the center of the shrines, every column stopped trembling, every roof, every sutra, and even the rat's bristles in the cabbage garden: there, down below, everything came to a halt once again, once again nothing in the foundations moved, tranquility reigned, and the earlier quality of silence returned to the monastery just as the thirteen stinking, withered, and nailed-up goldfish carcasses ceased their swaying; earlier, during that long minute, as if in some dance of death, together in rhythm, they had gently begun to swing to and fro on the iron nails.

XXXVI

The abbot's residence was comprised altogether of five rooms, each one opening onto the next. The rooms' dimensions could be expressed altogether in a few tatami, and due to the evident function of each room, they were fairly easy to distinguish. Approaching from the direction of the Golden Hall, along the covered walkway, the way led to a door opening onto a completely empty room, although, as an enormous ornamental lock barred it from outside, this entrance was clearly not in use. In this very small space, there was truly nothing: the floor was covered with six tatami mats; instead of walls there were movable sliding doors, fusuma, placed all around, all now motionless, strictly pulled shut, and on their soiled rice-paper panels, the battered traces of Chinese-style paintings could be seen. From here, the route led to a kind of office which was not much larger, conceivably that of the abbot: there were European-style desks, chairs, and cabinets on either side; these desks, chairs, and cabinets were all crammed full with dossiers, notebooks, file holders, modern-style published books, an electric table lamp, an old computer, a telephone, and a typewriter, so that the chaos reigning above at table and cabinet height was counterbalanced altogether by the tranquility of a heavy safe located below on the floor, in a corner. This room was not really closed off from the following one, namely the two sliding doors which could have definitively separated the two rooms had been removed; this section of the residence in effect elongated the floor plan, making it nearly twice as large, as if a signal were being sent: it was permitted to cross from one space to the other, as if it were important to be aware that the office and the other room that opened up from here—presumably a guest room where the abbot received lay believers, guests, and monks—were connected. In the middle of the room, a comfortable cushion covered with yellow silk designated the abbot's place, and around it, there lay scattered smaller cushions, covered with coarse unbleached linen, thrown about carelessly, as if the guests had just now arisen and left the room. Behind the abbot's cushion there was, built into the wall, a tokonoma with a thin hanging scroll: upon it there was written, in thirty-one characters, an enigmatic and irregular waka poem from the pen of the famous repudiated son of Kobo Daishi:

> The Buddha does not leave
> The Buddha does not come
> Search in vain, the Buddha is not here
> Gaze into the depths, look for nothing
> There are no questions.

Facing the wall yet another sliding door separated this room, presumably used for receiving visitors, from an even bigger one, the purpose of which, however, was difficult to ascertain other than for traversing this space when entering the abbot's residence from outside. It might have been a room where believers, guests, or monks could rest while waiting, or, judging from the low table with a cushion behind it, it also could have served as a kind of secretary's room, where one of the abbot's trusted subordinates could determine which visitors could proceed further, who had come regarding what matter, to decide who was in need of what, if it was truly necessary for the abbot to be disturbed, and so this might have served as a kind of retaining room, although it was also possible that it was simply meant as a kind of protective barrier between the official rooms and the room, located on the opposite side, set aside for the private life of the abbot.

Because in reality: from here, from this fourth, larger room, the way led to the inner residence of the abbot, into an entirely small room, the smallest of all five.

Instead of fusuma, there was a European-style door, and the lock was European-style as well.

Inside, there were objects crammed everywhere, immeasurable chaos.

The most disparate kinds of objects lay heaped on top of each other topsy-turvy: offering gifts, a pile of sake glasses, books and illustrated magazines on the floor, a large American film poster on the wall, an unmade bed, and facing the bed on a shelf affixed to the wall, a primitive television set fitted with a V-shaped antenna, a wristwatch and telephone also lying on the floor, trousers and shirts and socks and shoes all mixed together with innumerable dōgi and service kimonos for everyday use with belts, tabi, and geta, newspapers, plates, chopsticks and letters, envelopes and advertisement-covered plastic bags lying everywhere, the chaos of Babel, a mess that could never be cleaned up, the secret locale of the everyday life of an abbot, which was, generally speaking, secluded from the world in the most rigorous fashion possible.

In the middle of the room there was a low small table, and among the dried-out glasses standing on it were four large bottles of Johnny Walker. Three of them were already completely empty, the fourth was only one-third full.

The abbot could have been in a hurry when he left.

He had forgotten to screw the cap back onto the bottle.

The entire tiny room stank of whiskey.

On the unmade bed—just as if he had been in the middle of reading, exactly at that point when someone, because of some sort of immediate reason, stops reading, and temporarily, and therefore carelessly, tosses the volume aside—there lay a French book, opened largely at the middle with the spine facing upward, and truly thrown onto the blanket. The title, which could be seen on the spine, read as follows: *The Infinite Mistake*. The author of this volume was one Sir Wilford Stanley Gilmore.

XXXVII

The grandson of Prince Genji folded his hands in prayer and bowed twice, deeply, toward the Golden Hall.

He turned neither to the exit nor toward the gates, but back, to the right side of the monastery.

He was hoping that even if everything here was completely depopulated, he would still be able to find the abbot of the monastery in his place.

He stood in front of the abbot's residence where an inscription designated the entrance, cleared his throat, and uttered a quiet greeting.

He received no answer, and so he tried, cautiously, to pull the sliding door to one side.

The sliding door opened.

The grandson of Prince Genji stepped into the first room which served as a retaining room or waiting room, and stopped: he greeted the head of the monastery in a louder voice.

He received no answer.

The silence everywhere was complete.

He did not wish to make his departure without leaving a sign for the head of the monastery that he had been here, so he looked around and decided to open the door nearest to him. The door closest to him, although he didn't realize it, led to the abbot's private residence, and when he pushed down the handle and realized it was open, he removed his geta, placed them neatly next to each other by the doorway, and bowing his head, entered.

There was no one in the room.

Then, in that first moment, without even having looked around, he thought he would look for a suitable piece of paper, a brush, and ink, so that, in a few lines, he could inform the abbot of his visit, and that he regretted that their meeting, which he had been looking forward to with such hope, could not, at this time, take place.

Then he was stopped in his tracks on the threshold.

He looked all around at the chaos, so unseemly in this place, of clothes and plates and eating utensils and dōgi and kimonos and geta and cups and whiskey glasses tossed on top of each other, he looked around at all the surprising objects in this room, his eyes were caught by the American movie poster on the wall, the television installed across from the bed, the telephone lying on the floor and the wrist-watch which he almost stepped on, and in his shock that he had found such a world as this in a place so ill-suited for it, and forgetting the obligatory courtesy and respect the situation demanded, he simply for-got himself, because he did not immediately exit the room, because he did not leave the whole thing there, because he did not shut the door to the private empire of the head of the order at once—as he should have done under any circumstances—but in his shock, slowly, like someone who could not believe his eyes, he took a step further into the room, sank down onto the bed, and, in his lack of attentiveness, almost sat on the book that had been left there, he took it into his hands, looked at the title, and confusedly leafed through it.

There was no sound at all, not even the slightest noise could be heard from anywhere in the building.

Outside, it had grown completely dark.

The grandson of Prince Genji turned over the pages of the book for a long time, then, marking with a piece of paper where it had been opened, closed the book cautiously and looked for someplace to put it in the room.

He moved a few objects on one of the wall shelves aside, and placed the book there.

He knew very well that what he was doing was rash and lacking in all respect.

He did not look for a piece of paper, a brush, and ink.

At the time of his next visit, he would certainly have to make amends for all of this.

But the grandson of Prince Genji wasn't thinking about that right now.

With a sad gaze, he once again looked all around the room, then he stepped out into the waiting room, slipped into his geta, slowly walked to the exit, then, pulling the door shut after himself, he cut across the courtyard with quick steps, and hurriedly left the monastery.

In the distance, near the two repositories, beneath the dense branches of the azalea bush, the rabid fox began to be seized by convulsions.

The fox was dying.

In those numbing, motionless, troubled, crimson eyes, no kind of frenzy whatsoever was burning now.

The light in them had broken.

XXXVIII

The work authored by Sir Wilford Stanley Gilmore was truly substantial, running to more than two thousand pages, and the publisher in the brief foreword, rather unconventionally, did not concede to mandatory expressions of politeness praising those persons whose support had made the present volume possible; nor did he adhere to the custom of wishing to recommend, to a general audience, this lesser-known scholar to his readers' distinguished attention, no, not at all; instead, employing a fairly harsh tone, the writer of the introduction objected to his readers' potential accusations, according to which the whole thing would have been more comfortable, more easily navigable, as well as daintier, if it had been published in two volumes, and with this invective, thoroughly unjustified, presented with no explanation—not to mention the startling openness of its formulation or rather its unconstrained tone (almost continually employing such expressions as "go fuck yourselves," "shit," and "your mother's cunt")—the impression was created that the writer of this introduction was not any kind of separate personage but none other than the author himself; for when a publisher— concealing himself within the third person singular—reflects, in a perhaps excessively original introduction, upon the extraordinary difficulties of the life and work of the "writer," opining that the publication of this work in two volumes—accordingly the arbitrary separation of the first volume from the second—would have in nearly microscopic size, quickly followed by the hundreds, thousands, ten thousands, and hundred thousands, but all of them, each individual number, according to the linear, strictly progressing order of the given series, then the millions, the billions, and the trillions, not omitting, leaving out, or skipping over—with dreadful precision and thoroughness—a single number, and only at the point when, after one thousand billion, the first trillion was reached, it occurred for the first time that the numerals were not conveyed in succession, accordingly the author did not write down the form of each individual number, but he stopped doing so with the understanding that he was designating only the measure of where he was: accordingly, he was now at one trillion, and so he wrote down 1,000,000,000,000, and then he added the next number, 1,000,000,000,001, appending the phrase "and so on," until he got to ten trillion, then one hundred trillion, one thousand trillion and ten thousand trillion, then he got to one hundred thousand trillion, and for these quantities he only conveyed the units themselves, so that for example, here, at one thousand trillion or one quintillion he simply printed 1,000,000,000,000,000,000 but he didn't continue with 1,000,000,000,000,000,001, but instead denoted the numbers: ten quintillion, one hundred quintillion, one thousand quintillion, and so on up till one septillion, always indicating the omitted numbers with ellipses, so then up to one septillion which contained twenty-four zeros after the number one and then on up till one nonillion which contained thirty zeros after the one, and he didn't stop, he continued with one undecillion, one tredecillion, one quindecillion, one septendecillion, one novemdecillion, and then a number which he termed unvigintillion, after which he wrote sixty-six zeros after the number one, and he went on, there followed horrendous quantities of zeros from one trevigintillion to one quinvigintillion, then he got to one centillion, and there followed one million centillion, one billion centillion, one trillion centillion, one quintillion centillion, and finally, after one undecicentillion

centillion, there followed one undecicentillion duocentillion, and from there, toward the end of the book there ensued the following shocking number, which, even if he did not denote it with letters but only with numbers of course, as he had done up till now, namely, there then came the number of nine-hundred-ninety-nine-thousand-nine-hundred-ninety-nine-undecicentillion, nine-hundred-ninety-nine-thousand-nine-hundred-ninety-nine-duocentillion, nine-hundred-ninety-nine-thousand-nine-hundred-ninety-nine-nonaginta-tredecillion, nine-hundred-ninety-nine-thousand-nine-hundred-ninety-nine-nonaginta-nonillion, nine-hundred-ninety-nine-thousand-nine-hundred-ninety-nine-nonaginta-septillion, nine-hundred-ninety-nine-thousand- nine-hundred-ninety-nine-nonaginta-quintillion, nine-hundred-ninety-nine-thousand-nine-hundred-ninety-nine nonaginta-trillion, nine-hundred-ninety-nine-thousand-nine-hundred-ninety-nine nonaginta-million, nine-hundred-ninety-nine-thousand-nine-hundred-ninety-nine nonagintillion, so that here, with the usual ellipses, he indicated that he was going to jump forward a bit, namely he jumped forward by immeasurable quantities, then suddenly he informed his readers that from this point onward he would make use of exponential notation, but in each individual case the reader would have to pronounce the given number, because it could be pronounced by anyone who would read it aloud in the line of numbers, accordingly he wrote the exponential number "ten to the one-hundred-and-twentieth power minus one," and he announced that this number was the final pronounceable number in his great work entitled *Liquidating the Infinite*, as he here, for the first time, designates his own work, the final pronounceable number, printed in bold cursive type, so that its significance can in no way escape the reader, the final pronounceable number, because after this, the author, Sir Wilford Stanley Gilmore of the Gilmore-Grothendieck-Nelson Mathematical Research Institute, asserts that the line can be continued with "ten to the one-hundred-and-twentieth power *plus* one," then "ten place of the objective universe suitable for writing, there will be number one followed by number two which is followed by the number three all the way up to nine, so that in the meantime, at one point the set of digits from one to nine will flow from the last place going backward to the numeral two in the first place, then to three and all the way up to nine, so that in the very last line we reach the final result, which will be ALL THE NUMBER NINES that can be written down, with the smallest possible numerals, on all inscribable objects as can be found in the world and the universe; this, the author concludes his own revolutionary train of thought, is the LAST NUMBER, the largest number, and no number greater than this can exist in reality, because reality is finite, he informs the exhausted and shocked reader, we are able to construct infinity exclusively by virtue of ingenious abstractions and the nature of human consciousness, as the true immenseness of the quantity of the finite exceeds the imaginary possibilities and the grasp of this consciousness to such a degree, that, unable to follow this really existing great quantity, inconceivable on its behalf, it perceives that which, naturally, appears to be nearly the same as infinite as infinite, it is not, however, identical with the reality of the infinite, not at all, because only the so-called theoretical mathematicians—nefarious, evil to their core, spellbound in a game and not in any examination of reality—dared, with their abstract mechanisms, to make this claim, for example by employing such constructions that state, let's say, that there will always exist a number greater than the largest number, therefore according to them, this already forms indisputable proof of the infinite, the so-called refutation of his life's work, namely, of the thesis of this book, only that this is no refutation, writes the resident of the Gilmore-Grothendieck-Nelson Institute, this is merely a construction, we cannot, in reality, discover its validity, we may not prove it for the simple reason that reality does not recognize the infinite number, because it does not know the infinite quantity: as far as reality is concerned, the infinite quantity does not exist, because reality expressions, in the end returning again and again to one single name, but returning to it with indefatigable, inexhaustible rage, the name of Georg Cantor, the author's wrath boiling over if he so much as mentions Cantor's name, it is perceptible between the lines as the blood rushes to his head, because Cantor, he writes, is the one who—despite the precautions of a certain sober-minded Kronecker—sealed the intellectual world of the West, the history of the scandalously limited scientific thinking of the West—he, this unfortunate Platonist, this pitiful God-believer, this deranged person suffering from serious depression, managed to convince this limited Western world that the infinite exists, that the infinite is itself a part of reality, he, this Georg Cantor, who does not even deserve—as he writes in the last line of his book—for his name to be forgotten.

XXXIX

No one in his surroundings truly felt either his indispositions or his fainting spells to be surprising, least of all himself. Ever since he'd been a small child, he had suffered from so-called "extraordinary sensitivity," as the learned doctors put it toward the end of the Heian era, a sensitivity closely connected to all of the previous lives of the grandson of Prince Genji, as they expressed it; a sensitivity, as they put it, causing his organism to respond with a state of extreme agitation not only to events unforeseeable to others (for him, they were already encroached in reality): even the mere hazy contingency of a given event was enough, the slightest chance of its occurrence was more than enough for this sensitivity to destroy his nervous system. Namely he— the learned monks reported—was made unprotected not by reality but the possibility of reality, it rendered him defenseless, putting him at the mercy of more or less vehement symptoms of physical indisposition, this will always happen, for this there is no medicament, they said, and there is no therapy, just as there was none today either when the simple idea occurred to him that he could somehow free himself for half of a day from the imperial city, that he might, on this morning, somehow escape his retinue, that by means of some clever trick he might flee their presence, and, remaining alone, set off toward a monastery standing on a hill or mountain, a monastery in which—according to a young scholar who had turned up in his presence not too long ago—the garden he sought might be found; it was no wonder if this mere thought was more than enough for these physical symptoms to catch him unawares and begin to torture him yet again, for that is exactly what he wanted, for something real to finally occur—before, when he was still in the railcar on the Keihan line, it had only been a kind of slight, insidious, sudden weakness; then, reaching the monastery, it took the form of a sense of dejection with no clear object, then it became an increasing, an ever more stifling pain as he walked from the Nandaimon deeper and deeper into the monastery grounds toward the Golden Hall.

Yes, it was decidedly a kind of pain but—as always— without any source, starting point, or identifiable center, it only just gripped him, closed him into itself as if never wishing to release him ever again. A pain which, however, caused him no surprise whatsoever, for after the introductory signs he knew he would have to reckon with it, namely, he was prepared, and therefore the entire onslaught did not frighten him, and not only because the laws governing his peculiar life were also peculiar, namely for him, a certain kind of danger was already indicated if he did not find close at hand, in such instances, a human being, a kind of tranquility, and, let's say, as he would indicate in a weak voice, a glass of water; even the mere idea of this danger—if it could be termed as such—as unavertable was unimaginable for him, as he could always rely on there being some kind of person, some kind of tranquility, and, as it happened, a glass of water close by.

And he had no doubt that it would be the same now, although on this occasion, on the terrace of the smaller shrine, when he came to himself, he could have easily grown anxious, because there was still no one standing beside him. He felt this to be a great deficiency, because he still hadn't fully regained consciousness and now he really wished there were someone to help him lie down, to take care of him, help him to stretch out his limbs, adjust his head, to ensure his complete and undisturbed tranquility, and first and foremost, he wished for there to be someone at his side with, for example, a glass of water in hand—this was namely the first thing that the grandson of Prince Genji always requested after one of his indispositions, a glass of water *by any chance*, he would say, barely audibly, or he would only motion, and already they were putting it into his hand, and already he was drinking, and already he felt the strength returning to his limbs.

But he yearned, he wished for this, in vain, no one stepped out from the numb silence to be at his service, so that, well, his consciousness hardly returned precisely back to where it should have been—what could he have done, though, but to somehow start walking across the terrace, staggering, with complete uncertainty, like a blind man, leaving behind the lesser shrine, passing by the stone steps and gate of an auxiliary temple which floated next to him in a swirling thick fog, he could not see or identify anything anyway—stone steps?! stone gate?!—to merely cut across this heavy obscurity, to somehow get out, to exit from this fog, to finally see something in this dizziness, namely to find tranquility, at least one person, and that clear glass of water at last, somewhere ...

He was very happy when, after a few steps, he realized that the silk handkerchief that had fallen onto the ground earlier was still there in his hand.

Thank God he hadn't lost it.

The cool touch of the silk calmed him; nothing else could replace that for him.

because if, despite everything, someone, after all this, still took a few steps into the courtyard at the end of which there stood the shrine with the little house off to one side, then that person still would have no idea that a true garden was concealed here, for if he looked around, at first and superficially, all he would see around him was a courtyard which could also be called a garden, but which was really nothing more than a small triangle overgrown with grass and a completely dried-out old hinoki tree, a few tiny bushes, and some small puny trees, namely there was a certain liveliness to this courtyard, there was a small black pine, a small larch tree, and a small oak tree, there was a small camellia bush, a little tea plant and a small dried-out boxwood, there was also a little momiji, a small satsuki, a small maki, a janohige and a haran, of course, but all these plants, located in the first triangle of the courtyard, were fairly neglected, because the whole thing had to be imagined in such a way that if someone stepped through the stone gate, he would see that the courtyard, which formed a rectangle, was precisely and sharply separated, by a pathway running diagonally rightward, into two triangles; on the left-hand side, within the upper triangle, the above-mentioned trees and bushes were aligned—but carelessly, topsy-turvy, a little wildly, to the detriment of each plant and to no particular joy of anyone either—along with that pitiful, dried-out old hinoki tree; on the other side of the diagonally cutting pathway, precisely by its right edge, there grew a few of these little trees and shrubs, for the most part just a few modest branches, and here and there also lay on the ground, as it were from custom, one or two larger pieces of cut stone bearing a few edifying quotations from the sutras—accordingly, this was alto- gether what anyone entering the stone gate would see, then he would glimpse the shrine at the back of the courtyard, itself a rather unas- suming shed resembling the dilapidated little house at its side, with a protective grille at its center, a simple cowbell intended as a proper shrine bell hanging from the upper beam, and inside, in this small open

right-hand side of the diagonal pathway, in the courtyard's lower triangle, anyone who came upon it accidentally, and cast a glimpse in that
direction, did not, afterward, *want* to speak of it, the desire to speak,
the volition to say something about it, was annihilated first of all by the
garden, and that is why this speech was, as a matter of fact, so difficult,
this so-called finding of words and correct expressions, because the de
facto infinite simplicity of the garden—really now! because the whole
thing was, let's say, eight steps of moss carpet in the direction of one
garden wall, and, let's say, sixteen steps of moss carpet in the direction of the other garden wall, four times eight hiro, out of which eight
hinoki cypress trees grew, all approximately of the same age, and they
were tall hinoki, approximately thirty meters in height ...!—and the
fact that there was no kind of breathtakingly extraordinary plant growing there, no stone of any fantastical shape, nothing special, no spectacle, no fountain, waterfall, no carved tortoise, monkey, or wellspring,
accordingly there was no spectacle and no circus, and it had nothing
whatsoever to do with pleasantness, neither with exalted or ordinary
entertainment, in brief, that simplicity of its essence also denoted a
beauty of the densest concentration, the strength of simplicity's enchantment, the effect from which no one could retreat, and whoever
saw this garden would never wish to retreat because he would simply
stand there, gazing at the moss carpet, which, undulating gently, followed the single surface of the ground that lay beneath it, he would
simply stand there and watch, observing how the silvery green of this
uninterrupted carpet was like some kind of fairy-tale landscape, because it all glimmered from within, that indescribable silvery hue glimmered from within on the surface of that continuous, thick blanket of
moss, and from that silvery surface there rose, fairly close together,
with just a few meters separating them, those eight hinoki cypress
trees, their trunks covered with marvelous, auburn phloem peeling off
in thin strips, their foliage, bathing in vivid, fresh green, and the fine

lacework of this foliage reaching up to the heights, in a word whoever stood there and looked at this would never want to utter even a single word; such a person would simply look, and be silent.

XLI

I f someone were to look down into the depths, if someone were to
look down into the space beneath the earth—immeasurable, invisible, but not infinite—which, with its horrendous work lasting hundreds of millions of years—horrendous because immeasurable and
invisible, but not infinite—which had brought that moment into being, that single unrepeatable moment of the garden on this day in this
late hour of the morning while the grandson of Prince Genji, suffering
from dizziness, blindly hurried in front of the entrance, if someone
were to look down into the depths here, or if he became immersed
in wondering what might lie here beneath the garden, then he also
could have cast his gaze along the lower edge of the stratum known
as the continental lithosphere, he could have stopped somewhere at
the inconceivable depth of eighty or one hundred kilometers, namely
his gaze would be arrested at the boundary of the stratum known as
the upper mantle, for that extraordinary stratum, the so-called upper
mantle, was and remained the true birthplace of all rock formations,
because here is where the four minerals of great importance came
into being: olivine, pyroxene, amphibole, and phlogopite, and from
them—precisely beneath this garden—green marble and chlorite itself, differing from the four great minerals only in their granulometry,
but still truly divergent: because here is where the so-called accessory
minerals came into being, those extraordinary supplementary miner-

als that survived the assembled processes of inexpressible strength of the earth's development, the story of one hundred million years of pressure and temperature, of moving and breaking, dissolution and solidification, they survived it, which meant that a few truly special and enchanting minerals—among them, incidentally, the most wondrous zircon—survived unchanging beneath the protection of an otherworldly immutability without even the most trifling of mutations to its structure, although that certain pressure and temperature, that certain shifting and breaking up of the plates, that certain dissolution and solidification were of unimaginable strength and persistence, well, whoever might have looked down might have seen this, and he might have seen what was happening above the upper mantle within the earth's crust and its abysmal and monumental processes, when, amid the slow sliding and gigantic crushing of the tectonic plates, the crust, with its own largely uniform magmatic structure, was formed, only to find once again, within this structure, olivine, pyroxene, amphibole, and biotite, namely he would be able to see the gabbro that truly comprised this crust, he could have followed as, progressing higher and higher, so-called felsic rock was formed, including the famous quartz renowned for its extraordinary permanence, he could have followed as, in the gigantic fissures, the dolerite veins were formed, how the layer of basalt then rose up with its top layer of pillow lava and the so-called sediment forming in the merciless process of decomposition, he also could have looked to see how all this had been built up from the frightening depths leading up here to the surface, namely the sediment's top layer where water, wind, heat, freezing cold, and, of course, millions of bacteria had created a few meters' worth of soil, meaning, beneath this garden, the dark, fertile, soft soil designated by the locals as kurotsuchi or black earth—accordingly, whoever would have wished to know and would have been capable of really looking down could have chosen this path; but he also could have chosen the path which led to significance, the reigning culmination of divine thought in time and space—immeasurable and invisible, but not infinite—on the other, opposite side of which there stood today this dark, rich, and fertile soil, this carpet of moss, these eight hinoki cypress trees, this garden in this late hour of the morning, in that single minute when the grandson of Prince Genji, wishing for a place of safety, searching for some kind of tranquility, a person, and a glass of water, leaning occasionally against the stone wall, passed in front of the garden's courtyard entrance.

XLII

The retinue, in the meantime, seemed ever more hopeless on the empty streets of the Fukuine quarter. On every other corner, they came across a drinks vending machine, and thinking this would certainly help, they tossed all their small change into it, all of them pressing the buttons, and they drank, standing there in front of the vending machine, yet another can of beer: not only did this not help them, it worsened the situation even further, namely, they got even more drunk, leading them to an ever greater state of helplessness so that after an hour of lurching around here and there, an hour of wandering around from one beer vending machine to the next, they ended up in such a state that, forgetting even the dimmest memory of their original mission, they desperately began to look around to see who could be of assistance *to them*, although they would hardly have been capable of stating the exact problem: was it that they had no idea where they'd come from, where they were supposed to be going, who they were, or that they couldn't decide how they'd ended up in this place; in any event, judging from their gazes, everything awaiting them now was difficult and threatening, because—they were able to establish this much—there was no one to turn to, the streets were still perfectly deserted, not one living soul either coming or going, no one approaching and no one departing, when suddenly it occurred to one of them: at the beginning of their journey, somewhere in the vicinity of a train station, they had met up with some woman or other, well, now they had a plan, they had to find her, and so they set off, propelled at great velocity by this hope, and they even made their way to a more southern station on the Keihan line, they entered the station called Tobakaido, practically running and immediately besieging the railway employee, frightening him half to death, but they rambled so incoherently, continually interrupting each other, that the railway employee, slowly overcoming his initial fatal terror, decided to put them onto a train heading toward the city, perhaps returning them back to where they had presumably come from.

And so he did. The railway employee kept on speaking, kept on explaining amid unceasing, heartfelt bows: they most unconditionally must embark upon the very next train headed toward the city center, so that the retinue, as if they had been given some kind of command, the meaning and goal of which they had yet to interpret and evaluate, blindly obeyed; they got onto the next train, but then, when the train had already begun to move, it suddenly occurred to one of them that "on the way," as he put it, they had left behind the grandson of Prince Genji somewhere.

And the grandson of Prince Genji? — he kept repeating.

He kept harping on this until all of them finally understood what he was saying, and they were frightened.

They could not go back without him.

They got off at the very next stop: once again they had a goal, once again they had a clear task.

To search for the one they had lost, to search for and to find him, then to somehow return to where they had come from, to return to safety, which, however, for the time being—as they stared at the sidewalk in front of them, again lurching in front of the train station where they had already showed up before—certainly seemed far away.

XLIII

The story of how the eight hinoki trees came to be here began in the center of the Chinese province of Shandong, in a small hinoki tree forest near Taishan, where, after the formation of the trees' pollen sacs on the flowering cones, the pollen sacs ripened and burst open, on a suitable day when the weather was dry and the sun was warming everything up nicely and quietly, approximately one hundred billion grains of pollen suddenly emerged into the air, a pollen cloud raised by a current of hot air then entrusted, at high altitude, to a strong wind current coming from the west and headed toward the east, so that this pollen cloud was borne all the way across the East China Sea to the center of the Japanese island of Honshū, and then lowered down, in the form of so-called pollen rain, in a southern district of Kyoto, onto this tiny monastery courtyard, precisely finding the crown of that mother-hinoki tree, already dried out, which, however, was only waiting for this visit.

This fairy-tale-like story, namely, was true, although it would be more fortunate to speak about how all of this—from the hinoki forest near Taishan to the trees of the Kyoto monastery, standing, still alive, in the out-of-the-way courtyard—was instead the story of a miracle, dazzlingly terrifying and numbingly incomprehensible, for the entire process really only spoke of how there rose, into the path of this rising pollen cloud, in the most literal sense of the word, millions and been dashed into the ocean, sinking there, it would already have been enough for it to fall somewhere onto dry ground, because there, armies of snails, ants, fungi and various kinds of mold, awaited nothing else than their chance to destroy it, accordingly again: the end, the end, the end. If it rained, and the grains of pollen adhered to the leaves in the forest or the tree trunks, once again no exit—that horrific range of possibilities of their destruction was immeasurable and unforeseeable, it simply could not be enumerated, that horrific quantity of possibilities, which otherwise did, of course, annihilate the far greater part of the one hundred billion grains of the Shandong pollen cloud, because by the time it got to the monastery, the scale of destruction was simply appalling, the loss, by the time the pollen cloud reached that solitary hinoki tree in the monastery courtyard, was dreadful, and again and again: it was unbelievable that out of one hundred billion grains of pollen, one solitary troop—for that was all it took—actually reached its goal, and then what it had been intended for could occur: the pollen grains burrowed in between the cone scales, and awaited favorable conditions there—first and foremost warmth—for these pores to reach the micropyle, and then, releasing the pollen tube and finally gaining the inner substance of the ovulum, breaching it and, uniting with the ovum, a new life, of neutral gender, was brought forth, that seed was brought forth which, after ripening—a process lasting approximately one year—possessed, without exception, every characteristic of the hinoki tree it would grow into, the entire future plant, and from this point on the common story of this one hundred billion grains of pollen and this single hinoki tree was much, but much less dramatic, because the dangers awaiting the seeds were incomparably fewer, for them it was enough if they fell down somewhere nearby, and fell down onto a good place, after their spring ripening, and that is what happened here, from the approximately ten million seeds that had ripened, altogether eight seeds not only fell in a propitious spot, but directly on the very best spot possible, onto a so-called nurse tree located nearby, onto the nearly completely decayed trunk of a Norway spruce, the very best spot, because here was the greatest conceivable protection for a hinoki seed, for the germination and birth of the seedling, the tiny plant could proceed without any greater danger—although this did not signal a definitive end to the trials awaiting the eight little seedlings, no, because if fewer perils lay in wait for the seeds, even more dangers were about to ambush the helpless, defenseless, tiny, sprouting plants. There could arrive, after the mild weather, a wintry cold, and if snow fell onto the frail plants, breaking their stalks—the end. The torrential raindrops could also be fateful due to their weight as they plunged down onto the seedlings, striking them down to the ground: they would straighten up again, but then another enormous raindrop could dash the seedling right to the ground, which would, in the end, destroy its outer protective fibers or wash out its tiny roots from the ground which would then dry out—the end. Then there was the arrival of the great enemies, the earthworms, various kinds of beetles, the slugs which would pull the seedlings down beneath the earth where only fungi and bacteria awaited the execution of the final task, the dirty work, the mopping up—and this happened in millions and millions of cases, but it did not occur in eight cases, here, just a few steps away from the mother plant, for, from these eight little plants—surviving every further peril—in the end, eight enormous trees grew, eight enormous, wondrous hinoki cypress trees in a monastery courtyard, like the emissaries of an edifying sentence arriving from a great distance, with a message spreading among their roots, in their straight trunks, and the fine lacework of their foliage, a message in their story and in their existence, a message which no one shall ever understand—for its comprehension was, very visibly, not intended for human beings.

XLIV

The grandson of Prince Genji was extraordinarily beautiful. He stood, head slightly bent, next to the offering cauldron, pronouncing within himself words of farewell before the Buddha. His silky, glittering, black hair fell to his shoulders, gently framing his face, which, in its extraordinary beauty, truly resembled the beauty of his grandfather's. His smooth, unwrinkled brow, the white paleness of his face, the secret of the freshness of his skin preserved his youth. His finely curved eyebrows, his eyes, chiseled with perfect assurance, the straight, thin, slightly bent contour of his nose, his full lips—all of this would have been more than enough to arouse people's wonder, but it was as if the gods had been trying to fulfill at least one single wish of Prince Genji, for they placed, into the gaze of his grandson, everything that his onetime world-famous ancestor had known about the content of radiant beauty, the perpetual loss of which, the collapse of which, the fate of which he had so often lamented.

The gaze of the grandson of Prince Genji truly captivated all those who glimpsed him.

He was a manifestation of the truth that there was a place, on this earth, for human sensitivity, for sympathy and compassion, for consideration and benevolence, for tact and humility, for exaltedness and a greater vocation.

The sticks of offering incense had now almost burnt down to the end in the enormous bronze cauldron.

The fragrant smoke slowly became ever thinner and paler as it ascended, swirled, and wreathed toward the Golden Hall.

XLV

The particularly tiny spores of the pincushion moss rose up into the air after the demise of a moss pad whose location could not be precisely determined: it still, though, contained mature spores, however dead and dried out, which then, due to equally particular circumstances—more precisely, their extraordinarily tiny size, approximately fifteen micrometers—rose just as high as such a drifting spore cloud could conceivably rise, and where above, a high atmospheric current known as the jet stream circled the Earth more than a few times with this spore cloud as well as with billions of other drifting materials, viruses, bacteria, pollen, plant debris, and algae colonies, until a vortex of air lowered, so to speak, the entire thing onto the middle of the Japanese island of Honshū, so that finally—in the bafflingly complicated system of nature's ongoing dreadful happenstance—they were delivered to this protected and abandoned monastery courtyard so they could surround the eight hinoki cypress trees, now nicely germinating, and so both here and there, on a favorable patch of ground, with the plan of a future moss cushion, during the plentiful monsoon rains, they too could germinate, namely their immeasurably lengthy and particular story could begin—they could germinate, namely in the beginning, the so-called protonemas could spread out, then divide into cells, developing into a protonema colony which, covering a section of ground, would then, after a few favorable months, bring forth the moss plant itself—to denote its exact name, echoing its southern Indian origins, *Leucobryum neilgherrense*—and it did bring to life, one after the other, plants that were still tiny and very defenseless, with their tiny and defenseless leaves, tiny stems, and tiny roots, from which, however, there very quickly grew real plants with real stems, real leaves, and real roots, and in which sexual organs were created as well, male and female organs on a single plant between which, in one or another raindrop, the tail-propelled spermatozoon swam toward the ovum and merged with it, as occurred here as well, creating the possibility of sporophyte generation and the agamous plant, allowing us to return back to that place where this wondrous, aimless machinery was set in motion, back to the creation of the spore-containing capsule in which, under favorable conditions, newer spores endeavored to ensure that this story would never reach an end, that something would always be sprouting, and that this wholly inconceivable mechanism would be ever driven forward, ceaselessly.

Here, in the garden, the growth of the various and variously located moss cushions—obeying the laws of their kind and fulfilling their obligatory activities prescribed by both sexual and asexual reproduction—comprised, in reality, the one and same moss plant sprouting ever newer stalks that spread all around the hinoki trees, one day each joining perfectly with the others, creating one enormous, interconnected, silvery, thick, and immortal moss carpet, for this had been the goal from the very beginning, for everything—from the spores floating up into the air from the dried-out moss pad into the jet stream, through the fertilizing movement of the spermatozoon in the raindrop up until the formation of the unified surface of the moss cushion, gleaming opal in its moonlike silver—truly everything, every individual tiny event, turn, and success had led to this point; this is what it wanted, for those eight hinoki trees to be born within this dazzling silvery carpet of pincushion moss, for this enchanting garden to be made real in the world,

XLVI

The dead dog at the base of the ginkgo tree looked as if it had only lain down there to sleep. It gently embraced the trunk of the tree with its fatally beaten body, and such mild tranquility emanated from its chilled cadaver that whoever might have seen it would have believed that at least it had reached what it might have reached at the horrific conclusion to its life: final peace.

Only its stiffened legs bore witness to something else, both the front and back legs, as, in these final painful minutes it had stretched them out and they remained that way, they stiffened in that position, stretched out, transversely, crossing each other: of the two forelegs, the left was thrust forward, and the right backward, of the two back legs, the right was thrust forward and the left backward, and everything was slightly bent upward, as if from pain, into the air.

These four small stretched-out legs betrayed that the dog had not found final peace, because from the horrific solitude, from which it had arrived, there were no other directions than the one which led definitively into this horrific solitude.

And it was still running.

It gently embraced the trunk of the ginkgo tree with its now dead body, but it was still running.

Because, between these two horrific solitudes on these four legs thrown forward and backward, as they stiffened into the air, it was indisputably clear that they could not bear to stop.

They were still running, rushing, galloping forward, because they had to run, rush, and gallop, because they had to run, and run, and run, as if this could never, but never reach an end.

XLVII

They didn't find the old woman, but to tell the truth there wasn't too much of a chance of that happening, as they hardly dared to move from the proximity of the Keihan line stop, terrified that if they did so, setting off once again in this labyrinth of the streets, a labyrinth that had become exceedingly unfathomable on their account, they would never find their way back, losing the return direction as had occurred in the past few hours as well, so that now they took no more risks, instead they acted as if they were about to set off in this or that direction, they took a few cautious steps heading upward, but they kept looking back so as not to lose the station building from sight, namely, they got nowhere and they found no one, and particularly not the grandson of Prince Genji, about whom they had, in addition, completely forgotten about again, hardly one half hour had gone by, and they no longer even knew what it was they were looking for so much, again they had no idea who they were searching for with such passion, and so that is why one of them said, in a more decisive moment, enough of this, let's go back, at which the others approvingly nodded, and while they were just nodding and nodding their heads at each other, they kept repeating: yes, absolutely true, that's how it is, very correct, he's right, and so they went back, they got onto the next train, and as the train doors closed behind them, they collapsed nicely in a row onto the seats in the empty railcar, suddenly feeling themselves to be once again in a secure place, and they all stretched out their legs, loosened their neckties, unbuttoned the upper buttons of their shirts, then slid down a little further in their seats, and as the train sped up, reaching, between two stations, so-called cruising speed, they were already sleeping like babies, they all fell into a deep sleep, their neckties slipping out of place, their shirts crumpled, their legs, always yearning for a more comfortable position, crossed over the others' either from the right or from the left, so that by the time the train reached the Shichijō stop and began to brake, no kind of sound, no hissing of doors, no kind of annihilating singsong cadence of a young woman's voice over the loudspeaker could wake them up, although the voice was relentless, and in the ever more powerfully stifling stench of alcohol, amid the general snoring that was slowly filling up the railcar, it was relentless with its own inimitably patient machine voice as if explaining things to idiots, it just kept saying, and saying, with all the grace of lunar imbecility, it just kept saying, articulating each syllable merrily, as if this day had particularly been so sweet, and as if it were a matter of supreme delight that *Shimaru dooro ni gochui kudasai*, then nearly choking with joy that *Tsugi wa Shijo de gozaimasu*, then reminding the passengers, with glittering tact, that *Mamonaku Shijo de gozaimasu* and again that *Shimaru dooro ni gochui kudasai*, and so on and so on, never even noticing the stench and the snoring; it droned on, intimate, self-confident, with the inexhaustible strength of inane violence.

XLVIII

The grandson of Prince Genji stood in the entrance of the Keihan station. He looked back at the hill, but somehow from here he couldn't see it well. He looked at the street from which he had just stepped: now that street didn't even remind him of the one on which he had walked along before. He hesitated in front of the entrance to the Keihan line station. It was time for him to go, clearly, they would all be worried about him by now.

Yet he turned back to the street he had just walked along, and he began walking back.

This wasn't the street.

He walked up to the head of the street, and looked at it again, shaking his head in disbelief.

Everything was completely different: the houses, the sidewalk, the fences, the roofs.

He set off in the same direction which he had followed just now when walking down the hill. He was walking along completely different streets, although he was certain that he was not mistaken: he had come this way, walking back down to the station. At times he stopped, hesitating, examining the tiny intersections, the tops of the streets, sometimes he took a few steps backward, tilting his head to one side, and with the gaze of what he had seen before, he tried to evoke the houses, the fences, the roofs: this was a completely different district.

His steps glided gently along the pavement. He waited, but he did not sense the road beginning to rise upward.

He had been walking back for at least ten minutes now.

He should have been there already.

The streets were completely different, the houses were strange, wherever he looked, the fences were different, the roofs were different.

He was certain that this was the direction he had come before.

He reached the point where he should have already seen the beginning of the monastery wall, the bridge.

There was no wall or bridge. There were only tiny houses, low fences, flat roofs.

The grandson of Prince Genji did not go on any further.

He folded together the white silk handkerchief he still held in his hand, folded it in a square, and slipped it into the hidden pocket of his kimono.

He looked at the place where he had just been walking.

He looked for the enclosure wall, the bridge, the gate, the monastery.

Attentively, he looked upward.

Perhaps if the tiniest of signs were to betray it.

But all in vain: there was nothing there.

XLIX

The grandson of Prince Genji waited for the Keihan railcar at the station. He was by himself, and apart from him only the traffic dispatcher could be seen through the window of his small office, monitoring the electronic display indicating the routes of the scheduled trains; he noted down in his service notebook what had to be noted down; there was no one else, only him, with the white silk handkerchief still in his hand which he had taken out just now, so that he could put it in front of his mouth, and he stood there, with the white silk handkerchief in front of his mouth, waiting for the Keihan line connection scheduled to arrive now, behind him, there were only the two vending machines placed next to each other, winking like two awkward, good-for-nothing siblings, two vending machines: on one of them the red button meant hot, and on the other one the blue button meant ice-cold, they offered green tea and chocolate, seaweed soup and miso, beer and an abundance of energy drinks, the red button meant hot, the blue button meant ice-cold, this was all that stood behind the grandson of Prince Genji at the Keihan line station, only these two orphaned, dilapidated, unhappy vending machines on this particular, sunlit day which had become stormy in the morning and was now turning to evening, apart from this there was nothing, not a single traveler, only him, in his pale blue kimono, unmoving, his posture straight, pressing the white silk handkerchief completely tightly against his mouth.

New Directions Paperbooks — a partial listing

Kaouther Adimi, Our Riches
Adonis, Songs of Mihyar the Damascene
César Aira, Ghosts
    An Episode in the Life of a Landscape Painter
Will Alexander, Refractive Africa
Osama Alomar, The Teeth of the Comb
Guillaume Apollinaire, Selected Writings
Jessica Au, Cold Enough for Snow
Paul Auster, The Red Notebook
Ingeborg Bachmann, Malina
Honoré de Balzac, Colonel Chabert
Djuna Barnes, Nightwood
Charles Baudelaire, The Flowers of Evil*
Bei Dao, City Gate, Open Up
Mei-Mei Berssenbrugge, Empathy
Max Blecher, Adventures in Immediate Irreality
Roberto Bolaño, By Night in Chile
    Distant Star
Jorge Luis Borges, Labyrinths
    Seven Nights
Beatriz Bracher, Antonio
Coral Bracho, Firefly Under the Tongue*
Kamau Brathwaite, Ancestors
Basil Bunting, Complete Poems
Anne Carson, Glass, Irony & God
    Norma Jeane Baker of Troy
Horacio Castellanos Moya, Senselessness
Camilo José Cela, Mazurka for Two Dead Men
Louis-Ferdinand Céline
    Death on the Installment Plan
    Journey to the End of the Night
Rafael Chirbes, Cremation
Inger Christensen, alphabet
Julio Cortázar, Cronopios & Famas
Jonathan Creasy (ed.), Black Mountain Poems
Robert Creeley, If I Were Writing This
Guy Davenport, 7 Greeks
Amparo Davila, The Houseguest
Osamu Dazai, No Longer Human
    The Setting Sun
H.D., Selected Poems
Helen DeWitt, The Last Samurai
    Some Trick
Marcia Douglas
    The Marvellous Equations of the Dread
Daša Drndić, EEG
Robert Duncan, Selected Poems

Eça de Queirós, The Maias
William Empson, 7 Types of Ambiguity
Mathias Énard, Compass
Shusaku Endo, Deep River
Jenny Erpenbeck, The End of Days
    Go, Went, Gone
Lawrence Ferlinghetti
    A Coney Island of the Mind
Thalia Field, Personhood
F. Scott Fitzgerald, The Crack-Up
    On Booze
Emilio Fraia, Sevastopol
Jean Frémon, Now, Now, Louison
Rivka Galchen, Little Labors
Forrest Gander, Be With
Romain Gary, The Kites
Natalia Ginzburg, The Dry Heart
    Happiness, as Such
Henry Green, Concluding
Felisberto Hernández, Piano Stories
Hermann Hesse, Siddhartha
Takashi Hiraide, The Guest Cat
Yoel Hoffmann, Moods
Susan Howe, My Emily Dickinson
    Concordance
Bohumil Hrabal, I Served the King of England
Qurratulain Hyder, River of Fire
Sonallah Ibrahim, That Smell
Rachel Ingalls, Mrs. Caliban
Christopher Isherwood, The Berlin Stories
Fleur Jaeggy, Sweet Days of Discipline
Alfred Jarry, Ubu Roi
B.S. Johnson, House Mother Normal
James Joyce, Stephen Hero
Franz Kafka, Amerika: The Man Who Disappeared
Yasunari Kawabata, Dandelions
John Keene, Counternarratives
Heinrich von Kleist, Michael Kohlhaas
Alexander Kluge, Temple of the Scapegoat
Wolfgang Koeppen, Pigeons on the Grass
Taeko Kono, Toddler-Hunting
Laszlo Krasznahorkai, Satantango
    Seiobo There Below
Ryszard Krynicki, Magnetic Point
Eka Kurniawan, Beauty Is a Wound
Mme. de Lafayette, The Princess of Clèves
Lautréamont, Maldoror

*BILINGUAL EDITION

For a complete listing, request a free catalog from New Directions, 80 8th Avenue, New York, NY 10011
or visit us online at ndbooks.com